Three Little Words

Don Clark France

Rutledge Books, Inc.

Danbury, CT

ALL RIGHTS RESERVED
Rutledge Books, Inc.
107 Mill Plain Road, Danbury, CT 06811
1-800-278-8533
www.rutledgebooks.com

Manufactured in the United States of America

Cataloging in Publication Data
France, Don Clark
 Three Little Words

 ISBN: 1-58244-223-1

 1. Fiction

Library of Congress Control Number: 2002109121

Dedication

In loving memory of Emily Whitehurst Stone,

my college writing mentor.

Georgina

Very best,

Don France

In the spring of 1975, I was a graduate student concluding my degree in English at NYU. Whenever I made mention of this in the company of new acquaintances, their inevitable response was, "Why didn't you go to Columbia?"

My customary answer was, "Columbia requires more brain power than I have to offer."

The actual reason I never investigated Columbia was simply because it was too expensive. Mine was a checkered educational career which began with two years at Fordham which always resulted in the inquiry, "Oh, are you Catholic?" The answer: "No, I had a scholarship." Next question: "Why didn't you finish there?" Answer: "After two years it was clear from my performance that I should no longer be encouraged by a continued scholarship." Question: "Where did you finish then?" Answer: "City College." Invariable reaction: "Oh."

It was in this manner that I learned the huge variations in meaning of the utterance "Oh." Sometimes it had a noncommittal tone which meant, "In other words, you really only have two years of college." Often there was a ring of sympathy translating out to, "Poor fellow, you got fucked over by the educational system." On occasion there was a note of hostility meaning, "You reprehensible dolt; you had a chance at a decent education and blew it." Nevertheless, it silenced further inquiries about my academic preparation which was a relief.

My opinion of the MFA program was generally favorable except that, notably, the MBAs referred to the student body of our department as the "Masters of Fairy Antics," to which we, the admitted minority of straights, retaliated by dubbing the MBAs "Masters of Bullshit Artistry." That was about the extent of interdepartmental competitiveness at NYU since we would not be rivals in the employment marketplace.

In 1975, getting a graduate degree at NYU was somewhat like a progressive dinner. You just never knew where classes were going to be held. Some even changed location during a term. There was a reason for the educational anarchy. Some two years previously, the rulers of NYU had sold out the main Bronx campus to the city of New York for a community college. Unfortunately, NYU had failed to locate adequate alternatives for a number of its disciplines. Therefore, one class might be held in a palatial former conference room of a Lexington Avenue office building. At the other end of the spectrum, it was a filthy vacant storefront in Harlem with hostile lounging black men alternately glaring in at us or rubbing the backs of their heads against the windows making them slick with Dixie Peach Pomade. In between these extremes were edifices steeped in educational tradition such as the Jackson Heights Community Center.

During the last term of the program, it was impossible to avoid entering the portals of the lair of angry Dr. Harold Strikerman before leaving the portals of NYU to be admitted to the ranks of the unemployed. MFA graduates were virtually unemployable except for the gay contingent who gained sporadic support if they caught the eye of a well-to-do homosexual. I did not ever know the lesbian to straight ratio among the female MFAs, for they were a quiet and bookish and homely lot with the exception of Gladys Fishbein who lived out in Bayside in Queens and rode a vicious Harley-Davidson to class each day. Once, learning that I lived at City Island, she made the fear-inspiring overture—no, demand—that we begin to car pool. This was ridiculous. It was farther from either of our homes than to any class. I told her the lie that I was obliged to visit an elderly aunt down on West 84th Street each day after class. For weeks I dallied in the parking lot until the furious thunder of the Harley was inaudible above the normal racket of New York City. I still have not determined if I was more gravely unnerved by Gladys or the motorcycle.

Nevertheless, it was definitely fear which cowed all MFA students in the angry classroom of Dr. Strikerman. The first class session was a tirade which, in summary, pointed out the utter incongruity of an MFA degree and NYU. Next was an excoriation of Columbia University for their absence of vision in not recognizing his huge talent and hiring him away from the barrens of NYU. He had a new tirade each week—had lecture notes about them—concerning the ignorance and stupidity of his students and colleagues and a scathing indictment against City College to have had the temerity to begin calling itself City University. "It's just barely 'City High School.' Better it should have called itself 'P.S. City College.'"

Dr. Strikerman did cast out random assignments which were so integrated with his furious diatribes that often students missed them altogether; much to their subsequent unhappiness. The first writing exercise involved an essay in which we were to describe our home life. "We shall call it a get-acquainted essay," he stated nastily, making it clear he had no wish to become familiar with any of us. I had little grist for the mill, but I wrote valiantly and received a grade of 85 percent, the highest grade, I was later told, that our professor gave. He wrote the comment "I can't believe you went to City College." This, I learned from veterans of the program and even a few of the younger instructors, was a supreme compliment from Dr. Strikerman. A few were actually in awe of me.

My living was so very mundane, I was awed that I could make it seem a whit interesting in typed form. I had lived on City Island with my mother who was a very pleasant woman toward everyone except my father, a purchasing agent for a second-rate plastics manufacturer in Long Island City. Until I was ten, at which time my father wearied of my mother's abuse and filed for divorce, we lived in an unpretentious tract house in Mineola, Long Island. Following my parents dividing the sheets (MFA graduates avoid such terms as "splitting"), my mother bought out her two brothers' interests in her childhood—her late parents'—house at City Island and there we were. Mother was and is a CPA with a prosperous firm on Northern Boulevard.

City Island is one of those pleasant enclaves in the overall bigness and squalor which is New York City. One comes upon these oases usually quite by accident. The Green Point section of Brooklyn, where each day the women use scrub brushes to clean their stoops and sidewalks, is one of them. Almost all of Staten Island is a surprise. But City Island is truly unique. It is almost exclusively boat yards and yacht basins and crowded but well kept single dwellings. There is no sign on the short bridge saying, WHITE ONLY, but there might as well be.

So, obviously, I had a barren field of experience to draw from for an essay. My father paid for all my college expenses and my living was supported by my mother. I had an inglorious part-time job as a clerk in a butcher shop in the Bronx to pay for beer and Marlboros as well as the care and feeding of my rusting, city-brutalized Volkswagen. My mother had even gotten me my job with Sammy Shinbaum, the butcher, because her firm handled his books.

Sammy was a great jokester who, surprisingly, most reveled

in recounting Jewish jokes. Once he came out with a large pork tenderloin held dangling between his legs and crowed, "Bet you wish you had one like this, huh? huh?"

"How do you know I don't?" I countered. As long as I kept the money balanced and laughed at Sammy's humor my employment was secure.

Midway through the term, Dr. Strikerman got down to the big assignment. He did this by way of a screaming attack on New York City. "Despite the deplorable streets, regardless that this is a dying, crime and corruption ridden metropolis, for some unfathomable reason hundreds, no thousands, of the most renowned and brilliant artists: musicians and actors and writers and sculptors insist upon living here. It is your responsibility to locate one of them and develop a five thousand word biographical essay." We were all stunned. He added, "By next week, be prepared to report upon whom you have chosen."

A few of the class members grinned smugly. They were the handful from rich, well-connected families who actually knew some artistic celebrity. These students were, in the main, young men and women who had at some point flunked out of Dartmouth or Cornell or Smith and had continued their educational careers at NYU as a blind so their parents would be mollified and not realize their children were utter wastrels.

The remainder, the majority, of the class gazed at one another in vacant horror. We middle-class or lower, mostly denizens of the New York boroughs, knew no one who was anyone. For a musician, some of us might know a church organist. One student from the Bronx might, for example, live in the same apartment building with a municipal employee who pursued graphic art painting lines on streets and curbs with a machine. In my case, I called up the image of Sammy Shinbaum, the sculptor, hefting a half of a pork carcass out of his non-kosher cooler and, as he began to partition it, shouting merrily, "I'm about to invest in pork futures!"

My mother rescued me, as mothers often do. "Why, son, you can interview Zuma Alcorn. She goes to my church. I'll ask her next Sunday." At that point in my life I was a practicing agnostic; Mother was and is a devout Lutheran.

"I can't wait that long, Mother! Can't you call her? Where does she live?" Of course, I knew who Zuma Alcorn was; the star of music and stage and film, making a comeback after nearly twenty years of being a has-been. Making it big, too, in a smash Broadway musical named *The Ultimate Rainbow*.

"I'm sure she has an unlisted telephone," Mother protested. "But she's receptive to interviews. I know where she lives. I'll go by at lunch tomorrow and ask her." In that way I became acquainted with the lady who had been famous in the twenties and thirties and into the forties and then again in the seventies; the great Zuma Alcorn. It was she who drove to fruition this and another book; even inspired the title. I owe her a great deal which I am now attempting to repay.

Dr. Strikerman was less than encouraging. "Zuma Alcorn? The old song and dance woman who is trying to make a comeback? Is that the best you could do?"

"Yes, Dr. Strikerman. My family is not well connected with persons in the arts."

Since fully half of the class had come up with no one, he grudgingly accepted my subject, but warned, "The best grade you will receive using such a mundane, common individual is an 85 percent. So you can't earn an *A* in this course unless you yield to my optional comprehensive final examination which few students have ever passed."

"I understand," I intoned humbly, full well knowing a secret bequeathed to me by a graduated MFA student. Our professor had never taught us anything, therefore how could he test us upon anything? His seven page examination was a sham. Grades had to be submitted three days after the close of the term. I could churn out enough bullshit to busy him for days. My gamble earned me an *A*.

2

After just two sessions with Zuma Alcorn I had my essay, but I wanted more. I asked if I could expand my interviews, using a tape recorder, into a biography. She readily agreed, but warned, "I'm just an old woman, you know. I may repeat myself or get things confused."

I experimented with my tapes for some weeks attempting to create a biography. Finally, I retaped it all, deleting my questions and my responses, and there it was: the life of Zuma Alcorn. At least I thought it was. Ultimately I would use an entirely different tack. I am very sorry she did not live to read the entire story. As all America knows, eight years ago, she was killed in a single car crash returning to Queens from her coveted farm in New York State. She did, however, read the first five chapters and said dreamily, "I'll be damned. A whole book about me." Which it was, but this is the story of how it came to be. This was my first approach:

> *I am as old as this century! Imagine that! And in all those years, everything that's happened to me has had a happy ending. At least I've made myself think it was happy. Convinced myself. And it's kept me young. Now don't think there haven't been hard times. Ten years ago, I was living in lower Manhattan in a senior citizens' domiciliary. That's a fancy word for an old ladies' boarding hotel.*

I'd had to sell my old Chrysler, just about for scrap and it wasn't much better than that. You see, there was nowhere to park it and the last thing I could afford was garage rent. You don't leave a car, not even a ten year old Chrysler, on the street on East 23rd. Now that's funny! I'd hadn't thought of that 'til now. When I first came to New York in '21, I shared a little apartment with three other girls who were trying to make it into the racket. It was less than a block from that godforsaken old folks' hotel. What is it about the snake swallowing its tail? Or maybe "ashes to ashes"? Oh, the hell with it!

Anyway, do you know what I did with my first Social Security check! Hah!

I paid the back taxes on my farm. I was going to keep the farm, come hell or high water. Of course, I never told the senior citizen place I owned the farm or they wouldn't have let me live there. Not with a seventy thousand dollar asset on my books. I rented out two fields and made a couple of thousand a year that way. Then, too, little royalty checks floated in, either from late-night showings of my lousy movies or from performances of one of the five songs I wrote. At best, two hundred a month. So, you see, I was hard up.

This half of a duplex I own and live in here in Queens I would have laughed at back in the big times, but it's mine now. No mortgage. And the Olds coupe in the garage; paid for in cash. The last car I guess I'll need. God! That after ten years of saving up to ride the Greyhound up to the farm. You know, Mildred Bailey had a farm not five miles from mine. She hung on like I did, when times were bad. We were friends. That dachshund of mine, over there, is the great, great grandson of one of her dogs. Poor Mildred! Seven years younger than me, but dead over twenty years now. Just forty-four! She was too fat. She knew it, but wouldn't do anything about it. Of all of us, her voice—her singing—was most like mine. But she gave away her money. I was robbed blind from behind by my financial manager, the son of a bitch, Marty Abner.

It wasn't that I hadn't saved or didn't try to get work. For twenty years I kept trying for parts, but the answer was a variation of that song I made popular, "Three Little Words." Except the three little words became, "Go to hell!" And Marty had put all my money in investments that made him big bucks in the early years, but petered out when I needed them. Damn that Marty!

But let me go back to the beginning. All the way back to when I can first remember: Marion, Illinois. My God! That's where I was born. You know, most of we girls were from the Midwest. Helen Morgan was raised in Danville. There was a sad but mighty life! My age! Born the same year as I was and dead at forty-one. Before World War II, just when she had her life straightened out. But I'll tell more about her later. We were good friends.

Then there was Ruth Etting, from somewhere in Nebraska. No one could ever get close to her. But, Lord, she was good! Now, Mildred—Mildred Bailey—was from the West Coast. Oregon, I think. She was the exception. You know, she gave Bing Crosby his start, but I'll tell you more about that.

Another oddball, but, God, how she could sing, was Gertrude Niesen. Claimed she was born on an ocean liner, but I never believed it. She was all Brooklyn. I could tell. Another one, and I knew them all ...

So there was another approach to flush down the toilet. The story was there, a viable biography, but literately changing the approach from the seeming rantings and blatherings of an old senile woman, which Zuma Alcorn certainly was not, became a vastly perplexing problem for me. While the past troubled me, the present wasn't any joy to behold and the future stank. Of course, I could continue to work for Sammy and live on at City Island with Mother. On weekends when my mother was going through her severe moods ("What sort of career do you really want?" There is a lovely girl who has just joined our church. Won't you come meet her Sunday?"), I would, if my car was in better than precarious running order, drive out to Mineola to spend the weekend with Pop. That provided a forty-eight hour respite from admonitions about throwing cigarette butts in the toilet and drinking too much beer and not getting a *real* job or finding a *suitable* young lady.

The great thing about Pop was that he didn't care what I did. I could readily have taken a shit in the kitchen sink and wiped my ass with a dish towel or brought in a black whore without eliciting reproof. His negligence of manner was reflected in the scruffiness of the house and grounds and in its interior disarray. And Pop was always glad to see me.

One gloomy July day I was seated on a bench alongside Willis Avenue waiting for a crosstown bus. A few spatters of rain had fallen, but if I left the bus stop to get in a building's shelter, the bus driver, spying an empty bench, wouldn't stop unless a passenger was getting off which was unlikely given the mid-afternoon time and the grim neighborhood. Initially, I hadn't been completely alone on the bench. A mottle-faced drunk with gray whiskers and an incongruous beret had been seated by me sharing a companionable silence. Without warning, he had puked on the sidewalk; I leaped away but still was unable to avoid a few foul droplets splashing on my right shoe.

"Phew! Shtinks," he had commented and lurched a few feet away to a door-facing of a boarded-up store, where he fell asleep. The hot wind blew newspaper and debris and the odor of vomit into my nostrils. All this was not lightening my cumulatively unhappy state of mind. "Go ahead, world," I murmured, "barf all over my head. A heaven-sent giant puke. I deserve it."

As if on cue, it began to rain in earnest. A heavy summer down-pour. I grabbed a piece of cardboard as it flew by and held it over me as an ersatz umbrella (ersatz being one of the words ingrained into MFA students, even at humble NYU), but it was a lousy substi-tute (lousy conversely being a term to be avoided at all costs), for the real thing. For entertainment, I gazed at the mound of vomit as the downpour diluted it and it slowly joined the other foul effluvia in the gutter. As I did so, I compared my life to what I had decided to name the Vile Pile, and found that at less than twenty-four years my essence was slipping into the gutters of New York City; worse, there was little hope of betterment. I was trained to create, but had bogged down on the only project in which I could interest myself: The Life of Zuma Alcorn. I, Roy Chandler, was a disappearing Vile Pile.

It had been a bad day all around. At seven o'clock in the

morning Louie DeJerolamo, the mechanic who had had the good judgment to drop out of high school at the age of sixteen and who now, though a year my junior, owned a thriving foreign car repair shop albeit in such a sinister section of the Bronx that he only accepted checks for work performed, informed me that both the clutch and kingpins on the Volkswagen needed replacing.

I had no reason to doubt Louie about the kingpins. Not traversing the streets of New York. Once, early in my MFA course work, I wrote an intentionally humorous piece about the city officials being in a conspiracy with the manufacturers of automotive suspension parts. Dr. Schwaub, the instructor, was not amused. She grudgingly gave me a C. Later, I learned that not only did she not drive, but her brother was the Queens Borough Council president.

Either the clutch or the kingpins I could have paid for, but the combination required my turning to Mother who uncomplainingly wrote me a check. Nevertheless, as expected, I had to listen without protest to both of her speeches, the one about getting a decent job *and* the other about finding a nice girl and settling down. The later recitation always perplexed me. Did she just want me out from under her roof? Or was she willing upon me the unhappiness my father, and presumably she herself, had endured? That particular morning I was in no financial position to verbally pursue my speculations.

This put me in an evil mood and I was ill-prepared to respond to the jocular shouts of Sammy Shinbaum. In fact, once I failed to laugh at an appropriate time, and he glared at me. All I needed was to get fired. The problem was, I knew I was supposed to howl and guffaw at all punch lines, but Sammy was recounting his telling of a well worn Jewish joke to his rabbi. I didn't realize second-hand tellings required mirth. "Whatsamatta, goy? Got ya dick caught in the cash regista?" He picked up a bloody meat cleaver. "Lemme help ya out."

I did laugh then. "Too late, Sammy. I already pissed all over your hundred dollar bills."

"Jesus, Roy! You got betta sense than to even whispa denominations of money in the Bronx."

"Yeah, and I know where the numberless unregistered Smith and Wesson .38 snub nose lives, too!"

"Atta boy!" Sammy rosy disposition was restored.

I liked Sammy. Rotund, balding and tattooed, he was a stereotypical Jewish storekeeper. But there was a toughness beneath the surface which I knew was the result of a twenty-year career as an U.S. Marine, including eighteen months in a Japanese POW camp. Often I thought his roaring humor to be a bluff, a way of blotting out unhappy, perhaps ghoulish memories. A generous man, too. Often he gave me meat to take home, the gifts always masked in a joke, like appearing in the doorway with one arm held behind his back, the other extending a package of hamburger meat, saying, "Think of me when ya eat this." And he certainly didn't have the trade to justify a clerk six hours a day.

The rainfall gradually diminished. No longer was there a trace of the drunk's puke, but I was elated to find that I remained alive and well. I fished in the pack and located an undampened Marlboro which I lit, then inhaled gratefully. There was a pale watery sunshine, but now I heard thunder. But, no. It was a fast approaching powerful and unmuffled motorcycle. It was headed toward me!

The machine of destruction slithered to the curb in an expert controlled drift. The rider yelled over the racket, "Hey, Chandler! What's happening?" The voice was rough but definitely female. Then I knew! My God, it was the Jewish Hell's Angel, Gladys Fishbein!

"Not much. I was waiting for the bus when Mother Nature chose to piss on me. How you been?"

"Not bad." She inspected me closely. "Christ, Chandler! You look like a down-at-the-heels store clerk."

"That sums it up pretty neatly."

"Yeah? You're not writing?"

"I'm having a dry spell."

"It happens. Where's your car? Haven't you got an old VW?"

I nodded. "It had major surgery. That's where I'm going now. To get it out of the garage."

"Fuck the bus. Hop on. I'll ride you over. Where's it at?"

Terror-stricken, I weakly told her, adding, "But that's too far and it's a rough section."

Gladys snorted. "Shit. A place only *starts* getting rough when I get there. Come on. Here's the other helmet." She held it out to me invitingly. With the utmost trepidation, I gingerly grasped the offering.

And, yes, I know I should right about here describe the appearance of Gladys Fishbein but, after all, a black helmet, a scuffed black leather jacket, tight green-gray corduroy jeans and heavy black calf-high boots don't provide much mental imagery. She had, however, raised the visor to inspect my dishevelment, revealing a face that, if not attractive, at least had character. Below her left eye was a small scar and her uneven complexion suggested having had a bout with acne at some point in her adolescence, at about five years old, I suspected. What was remarkable were her intense black-brown eyes. They actually exuded a zest for life and adventure and fun. But, too, tragedy and sadness lurked in them.

"I've never ridden one of these," I admitted, as she deftly fastened the chin-strap of my helmet.

"I'm the one who has to ride it. All you have to do is sit on your ass."

"How do I keep my ass on the seat?"

"Hold on tight."

"To what?"

"To me, you dork. Who else?"

"Where?"

"Just about anywhere. Try to cop a feel, I will elbow your

balls so hard it won't even hurt when your ass slams down on 156th Street."

"Speaking of that delicate subject," I said, noting the hard texture of the seat, and wondering if the progenies of the Chandler name were at stake, "please try to avoid potholes."

Gladys laughed wildly and gunned the motor. "Hah! You fucking male pigs think your precious cods are the world's dream come true!" She was yelling above the roar of the engine. "Well, Chandler, a Harley-Davidson is the great sexual equalizer!" With a scream of searing rubber, we were off, peals of maniacal laughter drifting back to me.

So, as Gladys' Harley walloped my genitals to an impotent pulp during the furious uptown ride, I discovered the answer to what had begun as idle, passing curiosity. Question: Why was this insane young woman, in the middle of a hot July afternoon, wearing a leather jacket and heavy boots? Answer: As I clutched her about the waist, my whole body beneath my sodden sport shirt, damp jeans and soaked tennis shoes shuddered with a Harley-made cold wind. Somewhere along Jerome Avenue my battered pack of three or four remaining Marlboros was snatched from my shirt pocket by icy unseen fingers. We cut through tenement alleyways and across the storage lot of what appeared to be a long-defunct warehouse facility. Then, quite suddenly, we were pulling up before Louie's battered establishment.

Clearly, all was not well. The mechanic's ample mustache was drooping forlornly and he was making imploring Italianette gesticulations with both arms to two men, one of whom wore a police uniform, the other of whom wasn't in uniform, but looked as though he should have been.

"What's this?" Gladys mumbled over her shoulder, "Are they about to bust the grease monkey?"

"Don't know. If they are, I hope I can get my car first."

I dismounted shakily and approached the trio. Until it occurred to me to raise the visor, I remained anonymous, but when I did reveal myself, Louie became abject. "Christ, Roy! Some motherfucker ripped off your car! I got the keys here. I had Tony park it just across the street. Half an hour ago. Maybe less."

"Oh shit, Louie! All I need today."

Gladys had nosed the motorcycle toward us so that now the front tire was a mere three inches from the ass-crack of the uniformed policeman. No one seemed to notice. The conversation was too intense. The plain-clothes cop pointed at Louie. "Look here, little crooked wop. Tell me. You runnin' a little snatch and strip business on the side?"

"No! No, sirs! Not me. Never before has... I'm just trying to run a' honest business."

I pitied him and said reasonably, "Look. Louie has been working on my car for five years. If he was a crook, he could have taken the car when it was three years old, when it was bought from the Connecticut geometry teacher, when it was still worth a fuck. The car." I concluded lamely.

Gladys gunned the Harley to get attention. Everyone looked. She said smoothly, "It seems to me, that you people are missing the point. Why aren't you out beating sidewalks for the car inside of brow-beating this ignorant dago?"

The uniformed policeman scowled, "Listen, sister. Butt out. I could write an improper mufflering citation for that bike."

"Fuck you! Blue-belly pig! I could be in New Rochelle before your fat ass could ease into that squad car." Fishbein was in rare form.

"Oh yeah?" her adversary snarled, advancing with light-footed menace. "How about I bring you in on disorderly conduct?"

The scene had attracted a number of murderous looking

Puerto Rican idlers.

"Clancy. Drop it," the plain-clothes officer ordered, looking around nervously. To me, "You got your license and registration, buddy?"

I nodded and handed the documents to him.

He started writing on a form, saying, "The rip-off got called in a'ready. You got fire and theft on the ve-hicle?"

"Yeah. It's not worth much. Why ask about fire insurance?"

"These guys, see, after they strip a ve-hicle, they like to torch 'em, too. For fun, I guess." He stopped writing momentarily. "Brandt Place? That's City Island, isn't it?" He looked up at me inquiringly, a small dapper man, about forty, who must have watched many George Raft movies at some point in his life.

"That's right."

"Why bring your car to this slum?"

"I've known Louie, here, a long time. We went to high school together for a couple of years. Besides, I work down on Melrose Avenue."

Louie spoke up, "I had it all fixed, Roy. I wish there was something I could do ta help ya."

George Raft announced, "Louie, here, won't be fixing a car for you for a long while. Insurance companies pay slow as shit on a theft." To Louie, "You got shop insurance?"

Louie shook his head miserably. "I tried to get some, but got turned down." He gestured sweepingly. "The neighborhood."

"I can believe that," I said fervently.

The policemen got into their battered blue-and-white, Gladys' adversary shouting, "Get a muffler on the bike!" as a parting shot.

"What now?" I asked the world.

The world as anthropomorphized by one Gladys Fishbein answered, "For starters, we haul-ass out of spic-town. Come on. We'll stop for a beer when we find some place respectable. I have a wicked knife in my boot, but I'd rather not use it. You look like you could use one; a beer, I mean."

*****

"Reingold. Draft. Not all foam," Gladys was commanding a skinny black barmaid as I approached with a fresh, unmolested-pack of Marlboros, which I was tearing open wolfishly. "How about you, Chandler?"

"Make it two," I agreed lighting my smoke, inhaling grate-fully. I had survived my second ride of doom on the motorcycle. We were in a marginally safe tavern on 151st near the Major Deegan Expressway, upon which we had so recently roared southward that my knees were still quaking. Gladys had careful-ly chained her machine to the steel shaft of a NO PARKING sign. I had discovered one relieving feature of the vehicle, however. On either side of the rear wheel were stirrups so my calf muscles could absorb most of the impact away from my balls except for the most pronounced and unexpected road craters. It was, I guessed, akin to horseback riding.

"Never mind, Chandler," she said as I started to take out my wallet. "You've earned it."

We carried our mugs over to a table next to a grimy window decorated with neon signs, some of which worked. "Those are pussy cigarettes, by the way."

"What do you mean?" I looked around, but the only other patron was a fat middle-aged woman wedged in a far corner, fast asleep.

Gladys put her beer mug on the dented table and, fishing in a pocket of her leather jacket, produced a Camel pack. "These are the real thing," she proclaimed, lighting one.

"Too strong for me."

A shrug. "Worst thing can happen is cancer. That's what got my old man, but at least he had the guts to stay around and find out how his life was going to turn out."

"What do you mean?"

"Not like my old lady. When I was eight she drank a bottle of toilet bowl cleaner."

"That's horrible!"

"Tell me about it! She had the cleanest dead insides in Brooklyn. That's where we lived then. Christ, it's hot in here!"

She was about to give me two surprises in removing her helmet and jacket. First was her long exquisite wavy chestnut hair; the second was a gorgeous body: full breasted, slim-waisted, flaring hips.

To cover up my observations, I asked, "Why is it Jewish people are always saying 'Christ' and 'Jesus?'"

"In the first place, I'm not a Jew. I'm an atheist. Second, they make good expressions. Then, too, Jews believe in Jesus; they just don't believe he was God incarnate or the son of God. They won't fall for the specious premise that God dispensed a drop of holy semen in little Mary. I suppose you're a good Presbyterian, huh?"

"My mother is a Lutheran. I'm an agnostic at the moment,

but the day's events are pushing me toward your philosophy."

We both drained our glasses. She said, "And you've just noticed Fishbein has got a pretty good bod, right?"

"You have pretty hair," I said evasively, "I've never seen you with the helmet off."

"Sure, Chandler." She gave a short derisive laugh, turned toward the bar and yelled, "Hey, Sadie Mae! Two more up!"

"Not till you bring back them mugs you a'ready got. Boss don't 'low more 'en one out at the time."

"He won't like the way I send 'em up. We want two *cold* mugs. You got it? And as soon as I leave you can call me 'honkie bitch' all night if you feel like it. But be sure it's after I leave. You don't want to tangle with me. You Afro-Americans have been oppressed for three hundred years. We Jewish-Americans have three *thousand* years under *our* belts!"

"You have a winning personality, Fishbein."

"What are you going to do for wheels? How about getting a bike?" she asked, mistakenly thinking I might be a convert to two-wheeled conveyance. "I can get you a good used one for a thousand or so."

"A thousand! I'll be lucky to get five hundred from the insurance settlement, and God knows how long I'll have to wait for that."

"How do you plan to get around?"

"Around, hell. I'm just worried about getting home."

"That's no problem. I'll take you." She flicked her wrist in her first girlish gesture I had seen. Incredible, I thought, what handsome womanly flesh could be masked by a motorcycle jacket. "City Island is a long way from Bayshore."

"I don't live in Bayshore any more. Just over in Astoria, a couple of blocks off Northern Boulevard."

"Then that would be even farther. When did you move?"

"Don't worry, Chandler, I feel like a ride. I moved the first of

June when my fat, ugly scag of a sister got married. That was my wedding present. All the family furniture which wasn't all that great, and no more me."

"You don't like your sister?"

"Hell, no. I just feel sorry for old Irv Kornhauser, the poor turd that married her. Either she had a cunt that grabs like a snapping turtle or the guy's a masochist. I wouldn't know which; maybe it's both."

"So you moved."

"Yeah. A one bedroom walk-up. Third floor. Pretty nice. Now, what about wheels?"

I frowned. "Well, there is the ultra-reliable New York Transit Authority. And if it's somewhere safe, like my going out to my father's in Mineola, I can borrow 'Our Lady of the Garage.'"

"What's that?"

"Mother's Pontiac. The only five-year-old car in the city with all of its hubcaps and not a single dent. You could just give me a ride to Mother's office. It's on Northern Boulevard. I could catch a ride home with her."

"Is that what you want?" Gladys sounded offended.

"Just trying to save you trouble."

"How come you're so broke? I had you pegged for a rich gentile. What do you do?"

"A clerk at Sammy Shinbaum's Kosher Meats. Since you're an atheist, you'll be pleased to know he has a gentile meat freezer, too."

"Jesus, Chandler, you besmirch the hallowed name of NYU."

"What are you doing, les belle lettres?"

"Writing poetry. I just finished my first collection."

"Poetry?" I sounded as disgusted as I felt. I hated poems. I had wallowed through as few tedious and dull poetry courses as was permissible.

"Don't knock it. There are side benefits."

"Like?"

"You know the song 'All Our Love'?"

"Sure. They play it all the time. So?"

"I wrote the lyrics. I've made six thousand so far on that song alone in two months. Monday I go down to the anus of Manhattan to pick up some more demo records. It's big business. Fast profits."

"I'll be damned."

Gladys got our beer and, sitting down, her eyes brightened. "You want to go with me to a party tonight?"

"Party? No, thanks. This has been a bad day. Besides, I look like a derelict. What kind of party?" It was an honest question. What kind of party could Gladys be a party to? My loins stirred picturing this voluptuous creature, now just across a table from me, engaged in life-or-death mud wrestling. I saw her hair and the small scar beneath her eye encrusted with gritty dirt as she arose victorious.

"Big shit. I take you home. Then you can shower, change, put on your face—I mean shave—and we go back to Astoria. Just like that. See?"

"That's a lot of travel. Are you actually asking me for a date, Fishbein?"

"Date. I guess, if you want your male chauvinistic sap to rise, I am. If it appeals to your macho image, then yeah, a date."

"Where is the party? What kind is it?"

"Christ, Chandler. Just a party. You know. Drink beer, talk shit, laugh, smoke weed if you want to and bring your own dope. They're all just guys like us. It's in a neighbor's apartment. In my building. You want I should call out the guest list for you?"

"No. I have a pretty good picture. OK."

"How come you're not writing. Seems to me you were one of the brilliant lights at NYU." Fishbein kept you alert. She could change conversational gears instantly.

"I'm bogged down on a piece. Don't know where I want it to go."

"So? Grab something else. Have you forgotten everything we were taught? When an idea won't take off, you leave it alone for a while. If you go back to it later, chances are it will work. When it won't, better you should forget it. You know that."

I nodded.

"What was it about, anyway?"

"A biography. An expansion of the interview exercise I did during our last term."

"Whose biography?"

"Zuma Alcorn. That may not ring-"

"Really?" Gladys seemed genuinely interested. "She's still fantastic."

"Have you seen her show?"

"Yeah. Twice."

"You don't seem like the type that would be interested in old performers like her."

"So, you're no good at typecasting. Truth is old music is one of my hobbies. Why don't you just do an article for now? Get it published if you can, then you'd have a dynamite writing credit. You know: Chandler—the authority on Zuma Alcorn. See? Where did you get your material?"

"I told you. I've interviewed her."

"You *know* her?"

"Sure. She lives in Kew Gardens. My mother made the connection for me. They go to the same church." That was one advantage Mother had in not being an atheist or agnostic like us. "I've got all the material I need. I just can't get the right approach."

"Do you think I could meet her?"

"Sure. I'm going over there Sunday night. Come with me if you want to. This weekend…"Oh shit!"

"What?"

"I was supposed to go out to Long Island; spend the weekend with my father."

Gladys looked at me thoughtfully, while she lit a Camel and then took a swig of beer. "Say, Chandler. I might have a proposition for you," she said quietly.

"Only the knowledge that a wicked dirk is hidden away in your boot forces me to offer no response to that statement."

She laughed, spewing out smoke. "Fuck you, Chandler! You think you got something worth a proposition? Go on; yank it out. Right here! I dare you!"

"Fuck yourself, Fishbein! And tell me what self-respecting Jewish mother would name her daughter Gladys?" Instantly I wished I could retract my question.

Her eyes filled with tears and she averted her gaze in the general direction of the Major Deegan Expressway. But her voice was hard. "No self-respecting one. That stinking name was my mother's only apparent legacy to me. But if we were in private, I could show you the scars on my ass and back. What I can't show are the unseeable scars from the days locked in closets. That's why the bitch killed herself. My old man found out what she was doing. He went to a judge and told him he wanted his wife either put in the looney bin or his daughters put in foster homes." She laughed shortly and looked directly at me, a searching look in her black-brown eyes. Beautiful eyes. Eyes that had experienced suffering. Eyes that knew triumph. "You know what name I use for my poems and the song lyrics?"

I shook my head. "No."

"Adeline Fishbein. So it will rhyme!"

"Catchy. You want me to call you that?"

"No. Fishbein will do. For now. Come on." She rose and stretched. I gazed at her figure of powerful womanhood. No other description suffices. She put on her helmet, threw her jacket over her shoulder and sauntered over to the bar. "Later, Sadie Mae." She slapped a coin on the bar. "This is in appreciation of your superb service and welcoming disposition." From the glare she received, I gathered the gratuity had been slight. While her back was turned I drank in the broad shoulders, the slim waist, the full but muscled buttocks and could not picture it scarred. Perhaps she had been being dramatic. We MFA types often are.

Out in the fetid, noxious Bronx air, a black cop was frowning, studiously attempting to complete a parking ticket form for Gladys' illegally parked motorcycle.

"What the fuck you think you're doing, Ray Charles? Can't you tell a disabled vehicle when you see one?"

The officer looked uncertain. "Disabled? Then how come it's chained up?"

"Cause I didn't want two hoods to come along and throw it in the bed of a pick-up truck." She proceeded smoothly, "I chained it to the sign so police officers who knew things would understand the problem. See?"

"Yeah. Sure, lady. Think it will start now?"

"I'm going to try it." To me she breathed, "Get on, Chandler. Fast."

Predictably, the machine started on the first flick of the key. "I'll be damned!" she yelled in wonder to the perplexed policeman and waved a casual benediction as we thundered away from the curb.

Soon, in what may well have been a land speed record, the Harley galloped across the bridge and onto City Island. "Tell me where to turn!" Gladys yelled over her shoulder.

I leaned forward. "Third right, then first left."

She nodded in comprehension. Then we were home. Through the windows in the garage door I saw that Saint Pontiac was ensconced, meaning Mother was home. I'd rather hoped she wouldn't be.

"Some place," Gladys said appraisingly.

Was it? To me it was only a tall, narrow, bad-imitation English Tudor house with a detached garage at the rear. The entryway was at the left side and the only windows which fronted the street were from the living room. Just inside the door were the stairs to the second floor. A tiny lavatory with a sloping ceiling was crammed into the stairwell. The living room was good-sized, as was the dining room, but the kitchen was cramped and outdated. At the rear was a small sun porch which we used for most of our meals. Three minute bedrooms and the bathroom were upstairs. Access to the basement, where the furnace and water heater lived and worked and where I had first, and with subsequent frequency, masturbated, was outside and down a narrow stairwell. It wasn't "some place" to me.

"Come on in. Mother has been bugging me for two years to find a 'nice girl.' Maybe you can temporarily placate her."

"I may not be exactly what she had in mind," Gladys replied absently as she chained the motorcycle to the stout elm tree in our front yard.

"Well, you're obviously female. At least I'm not bringing a fag home."

"Do you usually?" she asked mockingly, removing her helmet and shaking out her heavy brown hair.

"I'm not going to tell you, Fishbein. Just let you wonder."

She shrugged. "I've had my share of queers on the back seat. A fucking lesbian once. Just once. I had to knock her off. Just *wouldn't* keep her hands off me."

I unlocked the front door and ushered my Jewish atheist cohort into the gleaming, sparkling, lemon-scented Lutheran home of Helen Chandler. "Mother! Your son is here and I've brought home a charming young lady. That is, she brought me home."

Mother appeared in the doorway to the kitchen, a tentative

smile on her face. Fishbein strode down the hall toward Mother; she introduced herself, and did a creditable job of it.

"I was just making some coffee. Would you care for a cup?"

"She would rather have a beer, Mother. So would I."

"Why, certainly." My mother gave me a pained look and added, "If you didn't drink them all last night."

"Don't think I did. By the way, here's your check back. I won't need it."

"Why? Wasn't it ready?"

"It was ready for someone. I'll let Fishbein here, explain. It'll be a great ice-breaker. I've got to go groom myself. Party tonight."

I left them to their own devises, hoping Gladys wouldn't say "fuck" and that mother wouldn't say anything anti-Semitic.

"Here we are, Chandler. Home sweet home." I looked up at an unprepossessing, chunky, five-story apartment building of 1948 vintage. She was chaining her motorcycle to the frame of a nondescript, aging black Plymouth. The Harley, I noticed, looked ferocious even in repose.

"What if someone plans to use that car?"

"No one does."

"How come?"

"The battery is dead."

"How do you know?"

"Chandler, it's my car. Well, it was my old man's last car. I never got around to selling it. When I moved over here from Bayshore, I got Irv to jump-start it."

"Why did you keep it?" I didn't think so ordinary a car, or any car for that matter, would have sentimental value.

"I don't want to take the time to give a fucking monologue about Fishbein's life story, but I was just eighteen when my old man croaked. I couldn't legally sell the thing, besides I was in my first year at Hunter and I needed wheels to get to classes. All that was left after putting the old man underground and paying off his doctor bills was about twenty thousand which the lawyer doled out for our living expenses and college for me. Rhoda, my sister, didn't want to go to college, but got a good job; somewhere in a back office so none of the customers would have to look at her."

"Where does she work?"

She laughed. "It's a small world. Does the firm of Ackerman, Chandler and Julianno ring a bell?"

"No shit. She works for Mother's company?"

"Yeah. I just found that out at your house. Your old lady asked me if I was related to a girl named Rhoda Fishbein. I started to deny it, but then admitted it. She gave Rhoda and Irv a toaster for a wedding present."

"Trust Mother to be in good taste."

"Anyway, you want I should paint you a picture?"

"Of what?"

"The car, dickhead, the car!"

"What about it? It doesn't run."

"Just buy a battery and it runs good. You'll have to get two tires. The ones on the back are bald. Just pay me to renew the insurance and you can use it as long as it'll start. It's got a current license and inspection."

I went over to inspect the vehicle in a new light. Inside the upholstery around the driver's seat was shredded, the rear window apparently had a bad leak—the back seat was badly watermarked; the headliner hung loosely—and there had been a vicious attack on the dashboard padding.

"Stop acting like this is a car lot, you dork. As far as I can tell, it's your only show in town." Fishbein sounded irritable.

"It is," I admitted forlornly. "Thanks."

"Come on. I have to get ready."

The interior of Gladys' lair was not unpleasant. It had been painted so many times there were no longer any right angles in the rooms. The living room contained a shabby tweed sofa and matching armchair, a new Panasonic stereo system and in one corner was a large, battered wooden desk covered with a jumble of papers and books, obviously where she worked. Two framed signs were on the wall above it. One said in neat letters "FUCK YOU, WORLD." The other one was in ornate script and read "You know you are a genius. Write so the rest of the world will know." Above the sofa was a large poster of Adolf Hitler giving the Nazi salute. Super-imposed at the bottom was the back of a blond man presumably performing oral sex on the Fuhrer. Above the stereo was a color photograph of Gladys—completely naked.

"What lucky guy got to take that?" I asked, pointing.

"I took it. Time delay. Are you hungry? I am. While I get ready, take two pot pies out of the freezer and put them on a tray in the oven. And be careful. That oven doesn't have a pilot and it's a son of a bitch to light. There are matches on the counter. Get a beer if you want one."

She vanished into a tiny hallway at the corner of the living room containing two doors I guessed to be the entrances to the bedroom and the bathroom. I passed through a minuscule dining alcove, containing only a cheap metal-frame dinette set, and into a crowded but neat windowless kitchen. The sparsely provisioned refrigerator had everything Gladys had mentioned but little else. I managed to light the oven with only a minor explosion.

Back in the living room, I lit a cigarette and pulled over a grimy Martini and Rossi Vermouth ashtray and thought about the last six hours. It seemed as though more events had been packed into them than all the rest of my twenty-three years combined. I owed it to Gladys Fishbein who was at the moment existent only in sounds; the running water of the shower, then the high whine of a hair dryer, now silence. I picked up the most recent edition of the *New York Times Book Review* and noticed she had made penciled comments here and there.

Then from very near I heard a softly rasping, "Chandler."

I looked up. My God! Directly before me, clad only in an unfastened bra and pink bikini underpants, which did little to mask the dark bulging triangle of her crotch, was what I estimated to be five feet, eight inches and one hundred thirty pounds of lithe, muscular, broad shouldered, exquisite, incomparable, Jewish-atheist womanhood. My arousal was strong and immediate. When she was very close, she commanded quietly, "Pull them down."

There was no point in my asking what. I reached out and she turned her back to me suddenly as I pulled. I gasped in utter horror. All of her back and buttocks and her upper thighs were a mass of scars and contusions. Some had healed to a muddy brown, others to a livid pink, still more to various shades of crimson and purple. My erection wilted instantly. "Jesus," I croaked out. It sounded like a stranger's voice.

Slowly she walked away from me adjusting her panties and fastening her bra. "You believe me now?"

"I believe you." I felt desperately sad.

At the door to the bedroom she stopped but did not turn and said, "I just wanted you to know before...I just wanted you should know. I've never shown anyone."

Then she vanished into the bedroom and I was left to wonder what she had meant by "before." Was she feeling the same attraction that I had been feeling and fighting not to feel all day? Well, why should I fend it off? Did I care that my parents, at least my mother, wouldn't approve of her? My quandaries were interrupted by a shout from the next room. "Hey, Chandler!"

"What?"

"Check the stuff in the oven and open me a beer."

I went to the kitchen. I obeyed. When I returned with her request, she was pausing in the bedroom doorway, lighting a cigarette. She wore a red and white sleeveless blouse, jeans and low-heeled red sandals. "Well? How do I look?"

"Very pretty."

"Hah! Don't shit me, Chandler. Pretty is not an adjective

used to describe Fishbein. On good days, attractive maybe. Or even striking. Pretty? No way. Thanks." She took the can of beer and subsided in the armchair.

"This would be the kind of place I'd like to have. I think maybe then I could write. At home I sit at the same desk in the same room where I did seventh grade science homework. Not really inspiring."

"Come on. Stop making up excuses. Do the article like I told you. Just adapt it from your interview. Four thousand words is all. I'll read it for you. Then we study the LMP and start sending out. One of the journals will grab it. I promise. Get some confidence in yourself. You were the one in our class at NYU with a fucking genius reputation. Use it."

I was genuinely surprised. "Are you shitting me?"

She shook her head and smiled, smoke billowing from her nostrils. "See, I'm testing you. If you're as good as your billing, I want us to work together. I got a fantastic project planned for us."

"If it's so great, why not keep it to yourself?"

"I'll tell you that after I read your article. Your deadline is Sunday. Five o'clock. Delivered to me here. Now, let's eat." She brought the pot pies to the dinette table.

"But this is Friday!" I protested, "and if I can get that car of yours running, I plan to spend the weekend with my father. It's been two months since I've seen him."

"Big deal. It's been five fucking years since I've seen mine. Besides, you know most of the material by heart and you said you need a different place to write. Is there a typewriter out at his house?"

"Uh huh."

"See? You're all set. Now. Let's go party! You bring any weed to smoke?"

"No. I smoked it for a while, but I got high one night down in Brooklyn and almost hit a little kid with the car. Of course, it was after midnight and the kid shouldn't have been out in the street, but it scared the shit out of me. Never had a toke since."

"Stuff never had the slightest effect on me, so I thought, why waste the money? Come on. Party time!"

"What time does it start?"

"Such a question, Chandler! Christ! A party starts when *I* get there."

On the first floor, Gladys stopped beside a door which had the announcement, "114" and beneath that, "Higgins." There were the muffled usual sounds of a party in progress; conversations, frequent spontaneous male and female laughter, and the tinkle of glass. Something, though, was different. Then it hit me. The music! Every social gathering I'd attended in the last five years had featured loud rock music. These were old songs. It was this, I would learn, which was the one area of commonality that this otherwise diverse social group possessed. "That's Jane Froman," I said, surprised.

Gladys smiled and nodded. Then she grasped my wrist urgently in her calloused hand. It momentarily occurred to me it was the first time she had touched me all day. Ever. "One thing, Chandler. There may be a fag or two in the company."

"So? I was raised in this city; fought off fairies at NYU. No problem."

She gave a sharp coded rap on the door to the apartment. It was snatched open quickly, almost anticipatorily, by a prematurely balding man of perhaps twenty-five who grinned at Gladys. She said, "Hey, Sterling." Across the living room a young woman, whose nickname I would learn was "Tit-Tat," came toward us. Her enormous breasts immediately explained half her name. The rest, I would be told, was related to the fact that she sang impersonations of Sophie Tucker. During one improvisation, that star claimed that she gave tit for tat and she was entitled to a hell of a lot of tat for what she had to give.

"Jesus, Fishbein! You've brought a man." She looked more closely. "Christ! It's *the* man!"

"Shut up, Tit-Tat." Fishbein came close to blushing.

"I'm Tit-Tat. Sterling's wife. He is the only success here. Works for the city. Assistant personnel director." There was a touch of pride in her voice which she tempered by adding, "Next year he promises he's going to hire some city employees who will actually work. Go make introductions, Fishbein."

"First, I want he should know where the beer and toilet are. Then I'll deal with humanity."

The apartment was much larger than Gladys' although equally outdated. A long hall was off the entryway indicating two or possibly three bedrooms. Furnishings and draperies and accessories were tasteful and probably expensive. An enormous ice chest was on the kitchen floor in a corner. "Beer," she said briefly, pointing. In a corner of the dining room, a rather pretty black girl had passed out or, less likely, fallen asleep. Fishbein prodded her gently with the toe of her sandal and said evenly, "That's Rebecca." Her tone was slightly tinged with wonder, as though she were calling attention to a dead armadillo by the roadside.

We moved on, returning to the living room. The air was heavy with incense, perfumes, and smoke: tobacco smoke sweetened by its mixture with that of marijuana. We were approached by a very stoned, very handsome blond young man. "Well, Fishbein," he said liltingly, "you have superb taste. He must have one super wang to make you break your vow of celibacy." His arm slithered around my waist, making my stomach churn. "Do you?" he asked me.

I pulled away, saying, "I don't do much comparing, but the

only way you're going to find out is if I piss on you."

"Far out," he said dreamily.

"Jesus, Chandler! Don't lead him on. This is Hal Materno. He's usually much more subtle." She turned to him, "Materno, this is Chandler and I promise you that he is straight as a fucking arrow. Where is Bruno?"

"Still in the bathroom, I think. That's where I left him."

"I'll bet," Gladys said wryly and moved away.

Materno said, "Nice to meet you, Mr. Chandler."

"Same here," I called over my shoulder.

Now we were confronted by a tattooed, black-haired giant of a man. If this was Bruno, I would feel obliged to offer up my rectum for whatever ministrations he saw fit. Fortunately, I apparently wasn't his type.

"Hi, Bruno! This is Chandler. He's with me."

He smiled briefly and extended his hand. I put out my hand hoping that was what he wanted. It was. "Pleased to meetcha," he said, and ambled past us.

We were opposite the doorway to a darkened room, and heard sounds of rhythmic squeaking springs and, I guessed, a headboard thumping against a wall. Gladys said, "That's got to be Jo-Jo. Every party he smokes a pipe of hash and starts screwing whoever he has with him. Usually he has the decency to close the door." She yelled into the noisy void, "Jo-Jo! Where are your fucking manners! I bring a guest and here you are humping away with the fucking door open! This is Chandler."

"My pleasure," a deep voice panted.

Gladys pulled the door shut, shaking her head in annoyance, and turned to me. "Quite a mixture, isn't it? True Bohemians."

"I've seen worse. Right now I want to get a beer."

Back in the living room, having gotten our bottles of beer, the slumbering Rebecca had made a remarkable recovery. She was in animated conversation with Sterling and Tit-Tat. They seemed to be trying to convince her of something. I followed Gladys' lead and sat on a sofa. "Hey, Rebecca!" she interrupted, "I want you should meet Chandler here. During my original introductions, you were passed out on your ass in the corner."

"Hi! She said brightly and putting a glass of red wine down on a side table, came across the room, bent down and, to my surprise, kissed me. "I'm sorry I was rude. It seems I just don't know how to say 'no' to grass. How is it you know Fishbein?"

"We were in graduate school together."

"Oh you're the one!"

"The one what?"

"Rebecca!" Fishbein barked sharply.

The black girl winked at me and said, "They were trying to talk me into singing."

"Did they succeed?"

She shook her head. "Only when I'm high. I have to get in *character.*"

"She really is good," Sterling said.

"What do you do, Rebecca?" I asked. "I mean, when you're not stoned and being talked into singing."

She pointed at Sterling, "I'm his secretary."

Just then a bare-foot, bare-chested, chubby man of about thirty shuffled around the corner from the hall, absently scratching his armpit.

"Well, well!" Gladys roared, "If it isn't our Jo-Jo! The greatest cocksman in Queens just finished with his tryst!"

"The world, Fishbein, not Queens." He reached around into the kitchen and fetched a beer. After a long pull, he belched rumblingly and said to the room in general, "Fucking gives a man a ferocious thirst."

Tit-Tat asked, "Just where is the lady of the moment? If you've screwed her to death, it's your responsibility to get the remains out of my apartment."

"She is still reveling in the deliciousness of the finest orgasm of her life. I'm sure she will rejoin us shortly."

"Bullshit, Jo-Jo," Rebecca put in, "you didn't do a thing for me."

"Now, wait a minute. I don't want to come off as ethnocentric—within my sphere I have no equal—but among blacks, where the minimum acceptable tool is eight inches long and two inches in diameter, I simply cannot compete." He sounded genuinely sad.

"You're telling on yourself," Fishbein laughed. "But you're getting sloppy. Leaving the fucking door open."

"The young lady was in urgent need," Jo-Jo protested.

Tit-Tat rolled and lit a joint, then changed a record on the stereo. It was a re-recording of ancient Paul Whiteman performances with Mildred Bailey doing the vocals. She called over, "Sterling! Fix Rebecca a reefer. I want Chandler to hear her do Billie Holiday."

He obliged, even lit it for her, then turned to me. "Do you write, Chandler?"

"I try. Fishbein has commanded me to finish a piece this weekend."

"Do you like this kind of music?"

I nodded. "The article I'm trying to finish is based on a series of interviews with Zuma Alcorn."

"I'll be damned! You've met her?"

Gladys said, "He sure has. He's going to take me to meet her Sunday night."

She turned to me. "That's assuming you've finished writing."

"You will be," Sterling assured me. "Fishbein is an unparalleled manipulator."

Yes, she was! That was the reason for my vague unease throughout the evening. A party where people smoked dope, screwed one another—even homosexually—and certainly got drunk, were all well within the realm of my experience. But this gathering was disquietingly different. All these people were performing, interacting, at Gladys Fishbein's command. She was the director. No, the dictator. I remembered momentarily the Adolf Hitler getting a blow-job poster upstairs. Was it possible she viewed herself as a Jewish female Hitler who could command her world to perform base acts? All of them were lackeys; worse, they were marionettes pulling their own strings. Each was a slave.

What was I? The thought was unsettling. I had been ordered to write an article, far more forcefully than, say, Dr. Strikerman. And I had unreasoningly coalesced. Was I, too, being drawn into her web of rule? I was uncomfortable, perhaps frightened. Certainly intimidated.

Only Rebecca's performance allowed an odd peace. Amidst the smoke and noise, which would have been appropriate, Tit-Tat put an instrumental recording of "This Year's Kisses." She was marvelous. I could and did close my eyes and there was Billie Holiday singing to us. That incomparable, previously seeming inimitable, crackling but at once smooth alto voice was there in that middle-class Queens apartment. Before once again lapsing into drugged unconsciousness, the girl belted out a rendition of "Am I Blue?" again in faultless, soulful Holiday style.

After her collapse, which alarmed no one, Sterling said brightly, "Well, Tit-Tat, we'll have to settle for some Sophie Tucker." He sorted through a dozen or so cassette tapes, selected one, and put it into the stereo. She was an equally polished impresario in her own medium, although much of the ad-libbed Yiddish was beyond my comprehension. Fishbein and most of the others in the room roared with laughter. Tit-Tat began with Tucker's trademark "Some of These Days," then went to "You Can't Sew a Button on a Heart" and "I'm Strictly a One Man Woman."

Fishbein stood abruptly when Tit-Tat finished.

"My God!" Jo-Jo exclaimed in astonishment. "She *is* going to do it!"

"As a rare treat. For Chandler, not you, Jo-Jo, you pig. Got the tape ready, Sterling?"

"Ready."

Suddenly Gladys was transformed, auditorily at least, into Marlene Dietrich, belting out "Lili Marlene," then "Falling in Love Again," some of it in perfect German, and finally, softly, "I Wish You Love." It was a splendid performance.

Several new people came during the evening's festivities, all being admitted using a common coded knock, but none of the late-comers were introduced to me. Jo-Jo's woman of the evening, a mousy-haired, unexciting girl named Stella finally appeared, fully dressed, but looking as ravished as she no doubt was.

When Fishbein flopped down on the sofa, her entertainment concluded, I said in wonder, "That was super. I had no idea you could sing."

"I can't."

"You just did."

"I didn't sing. I imitated."

"What's the difference?"

"Singing takes talent. Imitation just takes admiration. There's a hell of a difference."

A hand stroked my forearm. I was revolted to see that it was Hal Materno. My skin crawled. He looked at Gladys and said, "Must run, dear."

"Later, Materno," she said.

He turned to me, "Later, sweetie."

I matched his bland smile, but said, "Very *much* later."

Fishbein studied me momentarily, then said, "You handled that pretty well."

"What do you mean?"

"He's Bruno's lover and Bruno is the jealous type. Good thing you didn't lead Materno on."

"I assure you I was just keeping myself pushed off from a fag. Never carried the scenario past that."

"You ready to haul ass? You have a busy weekend ahead."

"Whenever you say the word."

She stood and stretched. "Long day, troops. Fishbein and Company are out of here. Don't make so much noise I hear it on the fucking third floor."

In the corridor, she began stalking for the stairway. "Where are you going? The door's right here."

"That's stupid, Chandler. Go all the way up to City Island, dump you and come back? Then I get you in the morning? Come all the way back? Fuck that. Just spend the night here."

"That's a tempting idea."

She snorted as we climbed the stairs. "The only thing tempting is that my couch is fairly comfortable. I hope you'll enjoy it."

I shrugged. "You do have a spare sheet, don't you?"

As she unlocked the apartment door, she nodded. "Not satin, though. Sorry."

"I had better call Mother. She wasn't expecting me to be away overnight."

"The phone is in the kitchen. Help yourself." Fishbein sounded preoccupied with other thoughts.

"I noticed something tonight."

"What was that, Sherlock Holmes?"

"You never touched anyone."

"So?"

"You've touched me. Twice, if I remember correctly."

She drew furiously on her Camel. "Look, Chandler. I won't argue that maybe I touched you. I won't argue that maybe I like you, or that I think you have talent. But maybe that's no flattery.

The last time I consciously touched someone, it was my old man, at his funeral. I put a kiss on my palm and then on his cold, shriveled forehead and said under my breath, "Goodbye, Dad. Wherever you go—heaven or hell—it can't be worse than the way life fucked you over."

"I thought you were an atheist. How can you believe he's anywhere but underground? Not even rotting? Just bones, now?"

She averted my gaze, took a final pull on her cigarette and mashed it out. "Go call your mother. We have to get up early in the morning." The exquisite body, with the obscenely ruined back, left the room.

"I am spending the night here in Queens, Mother."

"I see." A long pause. "How will you get to Long Island tomorrow? To your father's?" She spoke the words "your father's" with the same distaste she might have used to say, for example, "the city morgue." And there was certainly no point in reminding her that since I was in Queens, I was already on Long Island any more than I would inform her that the body of water creating that island, called the East River, wasn't really a river at all.

"I've made arrangements. No problem."

"Oh." Another pause. "Well, thank you for calling, Roy. Now I won't worry."

"Good night." I hung up. Yes, she would worry. Perhaps she would be awake most of the night. Probably she would be visualizing scenes of lustful antics which simply weren't going to happen.

As Gladys had promised, the sofa was not uncomfortable and sleep came quite soon, although not instantaneously. I was unaccustomed to apartment living and the sound of the random comings and goings for business or pleasure of other tenants kept pulling me back to half wakefulness. Slumber finally won out, for although this may have been an average day in the life of Gladys Fishbein, the day had been emotionally and physically taxing for me.

I made one last conscious resolve: I would meet this peculiar voluptuous creature, at rest in the next room, on equal ground with no intent to trap or dominate her, but conversely neither would I be dominated, or worse, consumed by her. I was low-key, but I was strong, too. Then it was morning.

The odor of coffee and the angry banging in the kitchen brought me fully awake. I smelled gas, heard a small explosion which was followed by Fishbein growling, "Temperamental fucker." Then she yelled, "Chandler! Get up!"

"I am up." I put on my pants and shoes, all I had shed the night before, and went to the bathroom. Using some Crest and an index finger, I more or less brushed my teeth. Then I washed and dried my face, put on some Ban roll-on I found in the medicine cabinet and, after combing my hair, my grooming was complete. Shaving was out of the question, although I saw a safety razor on the rim of the bathtub. I kept a full complement of toilet articles and a sketchy wardrobe out at Pop's house, so I could do a more thorough clean up later.

The coffee was strong, and we ate refrigerated canned cinnamon buns heated by the lethal oven. Fishbein finished chewing and, after a swig of coffee, she lit a cigarette and studied me. "Some sexual predator you are. I didn't even lock my door."

"You didn't leave it open, either. Besides I was beat. Yesterday was not the norm in the life of Roy Chandler."

"Look. Around the corner and halfway down the block there's a Shell station. I already called them. They have a battery to fit the car. You could probably get one cheaper at a parts store, but this is close. While you're gone to get it, I'll get the old battery out."

"How about the tires? Are they hopeless?"

"Very."

"Is there a spare?"

"Yeah. About as good as the back tires. Why?"

"I thought if I could make it out to Mineola, I could pick up two recaps, leave the car, then Pop could take me to get it later. He might even offer to pay, when he hears my hard luck story."

"Hmm. Not bad. Not if you're a gambler. OK, let's go." Fishbein was a human dynamo, wearing an outsized sweatshirt with the sleeves torn out and stained, ragged jeans. And, of course, her motorcycle boots. Why I found her so attractive was beyond comprehension; at least for now. Maybe I would think about it out at Pop's.

After she installed the battery and deftly secured the tie-down brackets, she sprayed starting fluid into the carburetor. "The moment of truth, Orville. Will it fly?"

"You're good at this, Fishbein."

"I'm even better at getting them out. Hah! That's the first bought battery that's been in this car in five years. I'm turning honest in my old age. Go on, Chandler, spin it."

I turned the key and the old engine started promptly, but the idle was rough. "Think it has a fouled plug."

She shrugged. "Maybe. Or a burnt valve. Don't worry. It will go where you're going on seven cylinders just as well as eight. Floor it a couple of times."

I obeyed. There was a cloud of black soot from the exhaust, but it ran more smoothly. I lowered the window. "Sounds better."

She nodded, closed the hood, came and gazed at the dashboard, leaning on the windowsill. "The gas gauge doesn't work and I can't remember how much was in the tank."

"That's OK. I know where that Shell station is. I'll put some in."

"Try the brakes." I put the lever in reverse and hit the brakes. She expertly noted the pedal travel. "Shut it off a second." After she raised the hood again and, I guessed, added brake fluid, she came over the window once more. "That ought to be better."

My arm was negligently draped over the window ledge. Fishbein leaned down and put her grimy paw over the back of my hand—that same odd contact she had used the night before outside the door to the Higgins' apartment when she had told me there might be homosexuals in the party—a strange grasp that allowed - no precluded - any response. A semi-caress that called for nothing in return. Now she said softly, "Be careful, Chandler."

I started the car. "I'll try. Promise I won't put a scratch on it."

"Oh, fuck the car. I mean be careful to come back here. Be careful that..." she turned away and lit a Camel. When she faced me again she was smiling. "I meant be careful to have our article written. The one you've got it in you to do." She gave my wrist a final squeeze.

So I had many thoughts with me as I drove west on the Grand Central Parkway, then cut south on the Van Wyck and east on the Long Island Expressway.

The car wasn't occupying my mind. If all the gauges besides the fuel indicator were working, all the vital signs were good. A flat tire would be a minor inconvenience. Saturday morning traffic was light.

My thoughts vaporized in the form of questions, few of which were being answered. What exactly did this audacious creature known as Gladys Fishbein want from me? Did she want a sidekick? A confidante? Was she attempting to bolster my creative ego? Help me?

And then why did she touch me, however lacking in ardor, and no one else? Did she perhaps want a lover? Was she emotionally capable of having a lover? Was I interested in being one? To that I had a tentative answer. Yes, I had the beginnings of an interest. That had begun when she had shown me her nearly nude body exquisite from the front, dreadfully disfigured from the rear. Even that initial horror was beginning to ebb, adding character to her whole being. Making her a survivor.

Of one fact I was certain. Our lives were to be interwoven for at least some time to come. To what degree and for how long were still mysteries.

Near Roslyn, I exited and drove south into peaceful, familiar, rather boringly dear Mineola. The tires had survived.

The neighborhood where Pop's house and the home of my childhood was situated had aged gracefully in the years since my earliest recollection. In the past quarter-century, trees planted in the former truck farm stood tall. What had been modern simulated ranch styles, split levels and, like Pop's, imitation Cape Cods, had developed a certain character, partly due to age but also because of the imagination of previous and current owners. Additions and adornment had added individuality and integrity to each.

Pop's house was no exception. Since my last visit, he had had the shingle siding refinished in pale yellow with crisp white trim. In the front yard was Pop himself, disinterestedly digging up weeds. He didn't recognize the car, so he only glanced up absently. A balding, middle-aged, Long Island businessman. That was all, unless you could see beneath the surface as I could. Once he had been a joyful young man, Brown University, Class of 1948. Then ill-fated marriage, one son. A long, boring tenure in a mundane corporation.

I tried to look happy as I got out of the car. Pop tried to look welcoming, doing a better job than I. He rose, came over to me. "Sorry, Roy. Didn't recognize the car." He shook my hand, and grabbed me by my ticklish nape of the neck, as he had always done since my earliest childhood recollections. "Come in. Fuck the weeds. Where's your grip?"

"I'm on the lam, Pop. Traveling light."

"Are you serious?"

"Of course not. Would I shit you?"

"There'd be no reason to. I'd hide you." He laughed. "Where is your car?"

"A long story. I'll tell you when you're sitting down. The house looks good."

"Wait until you see the inside. Where did you get the car?"

"A friend loaned it to me." I said evasively.

"Some friend."

"What are you talking about? That piece of shit you drive isn't any better."

"Take a look." Pop gestured toward the carport containing a new green Lincoln coupe. He sounded proud.

"Jesus, Pop! You get a big raise?"

"Not much. It's a demonstrator, but this is 1975. People are worried about gas prices. I got a bargain."

We entered the house through the side door next to the lethargic, opulent Lincoln. The kitchen had pretty new flooring and the old enameled metal cabinets had been replaced. Now it was gleaming fake walnut and avocado green; a wall oven and dishwasher. On one counter was a microwave oven. "How do you like it?" Pop asked anxiously.

"Really nice!" I said, but thought about the old Chandler money, mostly lost in the Depression, the remainder squandered by Chandler relatives attempting to retain the Chandler standard of extravagance.

"Coffee, Roy?"

"Is it made?"

"No, but I can have it ready in a few minutes."

"How about if we get a cup in town? I've got to get two new tires put on that car."

"Sure. I'll follow you down."

I ordered two recaps and settled into the comfort of the Lincoln. Pop drove us to a coffee shop. "How long on the car?" he asked.

"About an hour, they said."

The restaurant was clean and quiet and lacking in any hint of personality. "This is fine," I said brightly after we ordered.

"You're full of shit," Pop agreed brightly. "Now tell me about your car. And all about that wreck that's getting two new tires as we speak."

"Recaps. I don't want to invest too much in a borrowed car." Then I recounted all my tribulations of the previous days, referring to Fishbein nebulously as my friend from graduate school. Pop listened without interrupting and I concluded by telling him that I could use the Plymouth as long as I wanted or as long as it would run.

"I assume this friend from graduate school that you slept with was a young woman." My father was no fool.

"Spent the night with, Pop. On the sofa. By myself. I thought you'd believe me, although I'm sure Mother won't."

"I believe you, since I'm not naive enough to think you haven't spent nights in other strange beds. What's she like, Roy? Are you interested?"

I paused because my father was asking me the same questions I had been asking myself since last night.

He took my hesitation as reticence. "I'm not sure how interested I am or want to be. She is a brash, brazen, powerful, outrageous, almost beautiful, Jewish atheist. Her unlikely name is Gladys Fishbein. How's that for a summary?"

"Wow! If it's accurate, that's all I can say."

"You would have to meet her."

"I take it your mother has met her. What does she think of her?"

"I haven't talked with her in private. With Mother, I mean. But I instinctively think it was negative."

"I imagine so." Pop looked unhappy.

"Roy...you're a grown-up man now. Have you ever resented that Helen and I didn't...stay together...you know, for your sake?"

My answer surprised even me. "No. Of course, I've regretted it for you and for Mother. For me it was kind of an advantage. Ever since I was ten, when I was with either of my parents, I had their undivided attention. I know that isn't the way the children from so-called broken homes are supposed to feel, but that's the way it was with me."

"Speaking of undivided attention, I forgot you were due to come here this weekend. My bridge group is playing tonight. Can you get along if I go out?"

"If you'll remember to change my diaper before you go. And maybe read me a bedtime story."

He laughed. "I meant, you won't think it's rude?"

"Shit no, Pop. Go have fun. Besides, I've got a deadline to meet. An article I am writing. I need to write today, then proof it tonight, and finish it tomorrow."

"Really? A deadline? With an editor?" He was excited.

"No. Not an editor. I wouldn't be as scared if it was just an editor."

"Who, then?"

"Fishbein. My slave driver."

Pop looked concerned. "Maybe this isn't such a good thing if you're afraid of this girl."

"I don't mean afraid, like she'll kick my ass. I mean scared I'll disappoint her."

"Oh, I see." He didn't look as though he saw. Glancing at his watch, Pop said, "Let's shove off. The car ought to be ready by now." He stood, left change on the table and paid the cashier.

I settled back into the Lincoln's cream colored upholstery. Pop gingerly turned the key in the ignition as though adders lurked among the vast array of gadgets. It started, a muffled growl. At the repair shop, he glanced up at the Sunoco logo, took out the appropriate credit card and paid.

"I've got the money, Pop. Here."

"My treat. Forget it." He gave a brief smile. It was clear that he was unsure about this strange woman, Gladys Fishbein, which was just as well. I was unsure of her as well. My only urge was an unprecedented need to write.

Back at the ordinary, remodeled, pseudo-Cape Cod dwelling on Arthur Avenue, Pop was saying enthusiastically, "You've seen the kitchen. Wait until I show you the rest of the place!"

In 1951, when the still-joyful Chandler newlyweds bought their first and only home it had contained a living room, dining area, kitchen, two bedrooms and the bathroom. This had seemed adequate and was for our small family. There was, however, a full basement and an "expansion attic," as they were called, with a long dormer across the rear and plumbing stubbed in so there was potential for two additional bedrooms and a second bath.

Since my last visit, vast changes had been wrought, as my father now proudly displayed. New pale green wall-to-wall carpeting and fresh beige paint graced the first floor. The second floor had been expanded, although the bedrooms were devoid of furniture and in the basement a big paneled recreation room had been fashioned. It too was empty.

"Do you like it?" Pop asked anxiously, as if I were a renowned authority on interior décor.

"Very nicely done. You going to start taking in boarders?"

"Not unless they're blond and under thirty. And female," he added quickly. "No, I did it for the resale value. I had it appraised after the improvements were completed. Believe it or not, this place is worth nearly ninety thousand, and we just paid ten for it."

"Are you planning to sell out? Retire?"

"Retire! Perish the thought! I'm just fifty-four. I ought to be good for another six or eight years at the sweat shop." His smile turned to a worried frown. "It's just…the house is really the only thing of much value I have to leave to you and…"

"You're not sick, Pop, are you? You don't have anything wrong with you?" I was alarmed and in that instant, I realized how valuable my father was to me, how much I still depended upon him.

"No, no. I'm fine. Really."

"I still think you must have come into some money."

"In a way I did. The mortgage was finally paid off last year and," he winked and poked me in the ribs, "I don't have a son in college any more."

I felt again the compelling urge to write. "Pop, does your typewriter work? I'd like to use it."

"Sure. I couldn't get along without it. It's a new one, by the way."

"Jesus! What isn't new around here?"

"Me." He chuckled and slapped my back. "Go help yourself. I'm going to purge a few more weeds, then make our lunch."

I remembered that of course my father would have a working typewriter, for one of his few noticeable flaws was dreadfully crude penmanship. He even typed the checks to pay bills only scrawling a signature that no one would believe read "Arthur S. Chandler."

There was no need in my asking where the typewriter was. Just because it was a new machine didn't mean it wouldn't be on the tan typing stand next to the neat desk in the newly carpeted and repainted back bedroom, bedroom of my childhood. Now it served primarily as an office, but there was a single bed and a nightstand upon which, I noticed, Pop had placed a sparkling, bottle-green ashtray in honor of my visit. Except for an after-dinner cigar, my father hadn't smoked for a number of years.

After an initial defiling of the shiny ashtray, as I collected recollections of the notes and tapes and research I had accumulated, I began typing. Since I had not wanted to spare the time or rely unnecessarily on the Plymouth's fragile tires, everything but my memory was on City Island. So, as I worked, I typed in question marks where I was unsure about facts such as dates and chronology.

At the bottom of the first page, the title I'd left space for at the top of the sheet of paper drifted into my mind. It wasn't inspired, but I liked it. I adjusted the page in the typewriter and typed:

ZUMA ALCORN: A STAR OF THEN AND NOW

I was getting somewhere. What I was creating was fresh and read easily. I was elated and the work went quickly. By a little after noon I was up to the present which would be easy to write. I had considered doing the present first, then going into flashbacks, but I greatly preferred the straightforward approach I had chosen to use.

Figuring the word count, the twelve pages I had finished came to about three thousand words. Perfect! What was left to the piece and the conclusion I envisioned was about a thousand or perhaps fifteen hundred words. Just what I had planned.

I smelled food and went into the new, flashy kitchen where my father was at the stove stirring tomato soup with one hand and flipping over a grilled cheese sandwich in a skillet with the other. He looked up and smiled. "How is your writing progressing?"

"Great! Better than I could have hoped. Maybe I had gotten stale trying to work in the same old place. This smells good."

"Bon appétit!" he quipped, putting a steaming bowl of soup and a plate holding a sandwich onto the small kitchen table. "You want a beer? There's a six-pack in the refrigerator. And take a look at that roast I got for us to have tonight. Or would you rather go out?"

"Here is fine. I thought you'd forgotten I was coming."

"True. I just got back from the store."

"You went out? I didn't know that."

"You were pounding the keys so industriously, I didn't want to disturb you."

Just like Pop, I thought, always being considerate.

"Well, believe it or not, the damn thing is just about finished. I'll red pencil it tonight while you are out, then retype it in the morning if I still like it as much as I do now."

My father was looking thoughtful. "You know, Roy, you're a young man now. It's up to you, but would you like to move out here? You could have your own room and bath. You might find it less..." He cast about for a word that wouldn't sound like Mother was a bitch. "...regimented."

"Thanks, Pop, but it's a long commute to Sammy Shinbaum's. It's not my career goal, but at least it's a job for now."

My father nodded and changed the subject. "Your Uncle Manny and Sylvia are coming up week after next. I've rented the usual cottage at Sag Harbor. Think you'd like to come out?"

"Maybe I can. I'll see. Let you know."

Uncle Manny, a goofy-looking, jocular man, whose name, incidentally, was actually Michael, was my mother's brother, and not my favorite relative. Nevertheless it spoke well of him that he spent as much, if not more, time with Pop as he did his own sister. My uncle was a prosperous real estate developer in West Palm Beach. One of the reasons for his success, I supposed, was that people took his foolish demeanor for vacuousness, which was certainly not the case.

I traced my mild dislike for the man back to the basement at City Island in my early adolescence. He was the first and, to my knowledge, only person who caught me masturbating in my hideaway. Not that he told my mother, in fact, he pretended not to see me; just glanced briefly around the bare cinder-block walls as though he was looking for something and left. But when someone comes across a thirteen-year-old kid on Christmas day, in a freezing-cold basement, with his pants down and his fist around his dick, it would be a reasonable conclusion that he is masturbating even if the person were actually as stupid as Uncle Manny looked, but wasn't.

Pop and I ate in peaceable silence. Finally he asked, "Are you planning to sleep late?"

"I don't think so. Why?"

"No particular reason. Since all hell broke loose for you yesterday, I thought you might be tired."

"Don't forget about the resilience of youth."

"Touché."

"It's a crock of shit," I assured him. "I'm beat. Have you still got that hammock in the backyard?"

"A hammock. Not the same one you remember."

"Of course not. I know everything is new."

Pop laughed, reminding me, "Except me."

"After I finish writing this article, I can't think of anything better, more suburban summer Saturday, than to take a nap in a hammock."

"Fine. Don't blame me if you fall out on your ass. I always do when I try to sleep in the damn thing." He turned serious. "Is writing what you want to do, Roy?"

"I was beginning to think it wasn't. Until today. Now I'm reaffirmed. I know I can write. It's a great feeling, Pop."

"I'm glad for you. I don't know where you get it from. Neither of your parents has an iota of talent, or imagination either."

"What I'm writing now doesn't take much imagination or talent. It's more straight journalism."

"What's it about? I mean if you want to tell me."

"Sure. I don't mind. It's a biographical essay; I guess that's the best description."

"Who's biography?"

"Zuma Alcorn."

"Really? I'll be damned. I actually met her once. When I was in the army. I guess you know she entertained the troops all during World War II. I was the one assigned to pick her up at the airstrip. That was when I was stationed at Fort Benning, Georgia."

"That's interesting. Kind of a coincidence." I knew Pop had spent four years at boring desk jobs during the war, which admittedly was greatly superior to the alternative, which was being a target for German or Japanese soldiers. It was odd that in all the interviews Zuma Alcorn had never mentioned her part in the war effort. I would have to ask her about it.

By three o'clock my writing was complete. To anyone who has never written with an eye toward creativity, I simply cannot express the quintessential joy which comes to an author who has completed a writing that is correct in all respects. There were elements of sadness without being maudlin, humor but no gaucherie, and a clear message that the writer loved his subject, only from afar. But one aspect was bothering me. Badly. Whom had I written it for? For myself? For Fishbein? As a tribute to Zuma Alcorn? I just didn't know and, as I settled in the new hammock in ordinary Mineola, I was deeply troubled. But my quandary did not interrupt nearly immediate slumber.

I would soon wish that it had. The craft of writing is not difficult. That is, unlike mountain climbers or deep sea divers who, should they err in any way, will likely break their fool necks or drown, a writer has a vast array of strategic counteractions upon which to draw and mount counterattacks. Writing is most akin to boxing, but it is emotionally draining and intellectually taxing. So, as I slept in the backyard on Long Island during a mild, unexceptional July afternoon, I had a series of kaleidoscopic dreams.

In one segment, my uniformed father was at the wheel of an olive drab 1940 Chevrolet talking easily with his rear seat passenger, Zuma Alcorn. What was remarkable was that my father appeared to be the age he was now, but the actress was far younger.

Then I was taking Pop to meet Gladys. We were climbing the stairs in the Astoria apartment building. The girl who answered our knock was clearly my Fishbein, but she was magnificently naked and, when she turned away, her back was utterly unmarred. Her face had delicate make-up and green eye shadow and pink lipstick—cosmetics I was sure she did not own—and only I seemed to be conscious of her nakedness. She looked questioningly at me and said, "Leave? But why should I leave? This is a beautiful place." And as she stopped speaking the building began to crumble around us and I was on the ground on my ass in Mineola, very awake, feeling sheepish. Pop had warned me about falling out of the hammock.

Judging from the angle of the sun, I must have been asleep for some time. I felt dirty and despondent. A shave and a shower, I decided, were just what I needed. Then a walk; I would walk to the park of my childhood. The same park where I had spent an increasing amount of time during my tenth year, just to be away from the wretchedly tense house. Then, presto, I had been whisked away to City Island. And once more I came to love the little house more than the park. Loved the man who was Pop, and who came for me each alternate weekend, arriving as early as seven on those Saturday mornings.

I didn't not love my mother despite the fact that she operated her home in stereotypical CPA fashion—efficient and quiet and orderly and boring. Mother trying to win my favor by buying me elaborate clothing, my least favored possessions.

After my steaming shower, I shaved using a brand new disposable razor. Pop thought of everything. Rinsing the lather away, I studied my appearance and felt reassured that I was a reasonably attractive young man with hair Mother always insisted was "sandy," unremarkable gray eyes that ran to green at the edges, a straight nose, and what was known as a strong jaw. And standing six feet in height, I guessed my mother was probably right: I should find some nice respectable girl and settle down. But the trouble was the only image I could draw forth was glorious Fishbein, with her heavy brown hair, walking across the drab apartment living room, with her handsome, high breasts barely concealed by the unfastened bra, and the pink bikini underpants. I laughed out loud. Fishbein settled down!

Pop was checking the progress of the pot roast as I paused in the kitchen doorway. "Dinner at six-thirty. OK with you?" he asked.

"Sure. Fine. I've been sitting on my ass too much. I'm going to take a walk, just down to the park. You want to come?"

"I'd better stay here creating culinary delights."

I felt slightly elated and guilty for it. But I wanted to be alone; to reflect as well as to think ahead. I walked three blocks along Arthur Avenue, the street my father always joked was named after him, and turned onto Valleydale Road, a name I had thought even as a child to be ambiguous. And there was my park. Not an impressive place, but equipped with a battered swing set and seesaw, a baseball diamond where eight or ten children were playing an abbreviated softball game, and along one perimeter were placed four concrete framed, wooden-slated benches full of carved graffiti. The one I chose to sit on announced, "Jennifer sux dicks." I wondered briefly if the statement was intended to be boasting or accusatory.

I lit a cigarette and gazed across the field to the backstop of the ball field. During my last year of residence here, I sought out relief and solace in this little oasis, away from ever present tension. I came despite a frequent nemesis named Charlotte something-or-other, a knobby-kneed, skinny-legged creature of perhaps twelve or thirteen who would corner me over by that backstop and refuse to release me until I let her kiss me. It was not many years before I understood that the girl had the beginning stirrings of sensual urges, but could not grasp that such longings were not yet comprehensible to me. I wondered had Charlotte whatever become a "decent" girl when she grew up? Or even Jennifer who "sux dicks"? I wasn't sure how I had turned out. Then I remembered my writing—my triumph—and my dark mood vanished. I trotted back to the house on Arthur Avenue, to Pop's house.

My father was in the kitchen when I came in, but our dinner was apparently in a holding pattern, for he was mixing a heroic Scotch and water. "How about it, Roy? One for you?"

"No thanks. I'll settle for a beer. I need a clear head for editing tonight."

He concurred. "No more than two of these for me. These are real bridge sharks I'm dealing with tonight. How about the terrace? I swept it this afternoon."

"Fine, Pop." I grabbed a beer from the refrigerator and a plastic ashtray from the counter and followed him outside.

We sat in companionable silence for a few minutes. My father seemed to be carefully studying a slender white birch tree. Finally he asked, tentatively, "Roy? I'm not prying. I never do. You know that; but what does a degree like yours train you to do?"

"Work for a hundred and fifty a week at Sammy Shinbaum's butcher shop. You wasted your money on college."

He chuckled. "You could do worse."

"To he honest, Pop, the degree is worthless unless you have some innate talent. I think I do."

"You seem to. What happens even if you do?"

"Ultimately, one of two things. Actually three things. You could end up being a clerk in a bookstore; or at Sammy Shinbaum's, for that matter. But normally either you end up being an editor or an author. The two sound antagonistic but they're not. All businesses have a need for raw materials, finished products and a method of disposing of the product, hopefully at a profit. So writers supply raw materials, and editors and publishers, which in small companies are often synonymous, process those materials into finished products. It's a business food-chain very much like your plastics company, Pop."

"Sounds like it. But you've left out the important part. How about profits?"

"Well, periodicals depend on a varying ratio of subscriptions and advertisers. Newsstand sales are important, but iffy as hell. Newspapers don't have to count so heavily on subscriptions because their primary profits come from advertising, display as well as classified.

"Book publishers' marketing is a whole different world when it comes to sales. Except for book clubs, obviously there are no subscribers for books and obviously no advertising, except sometimes books by the same author or of the same genre, so…"

"What is that?"

"Same type of book. Like mysteries or science fiction or even gardening. Anyway, book publishing is risky because it's expensive. Publishing one or two turkeys can bankrupt a small company. The big houses have full sales staffs who call primarily on bookstores and libraries. Smaller firms rely on direct mail sales or the equivalent of manufacturers' representatives who travel around with the lists of several publishers or a combination of both approaches."

"Sounds complicated." Pop drained his glass and rose. "We have time for another drink before dinner. Get you a beer?"

"That, or I'll get my own and mix a drink for you."

"Thanks, but no. I've got to uncover the roast and let it stand for a few minutes before I slice it." He reached out for my empty bottle. I handed it to him.

Pop prepared tasty, flamboyant, occasionally too heavy, meals. He had become a good cook. My mother was a tentative, recipe-following type. What she prepared was exacting, but often delicate and sometimes unsatisfying. She cooked like she was preparing IRS forms. It was her nature.

So, as I greedily ate the slabs of pot roast, heavily seasoned in Worcestershire sauce, onion and garlic, accompanied by boiled potatoes and carrots, I understood how very different my parents were from one another. Why was it that food was a meter of likeness or difference between a man and a woman; an ex-wife and ex-husband? Well, for one thing, the human animal has only four basic areas for comparison. Those are eating, sleeping, defecating and copulating. I had no idea what either of them did or had done about the latter three, so the only thing left was culinary art. Each did that with their own flare or lack of it.

Except for glancing occasionally at the wall clock, Pop only looked up at me once. "Is everything all right?" He sounded worried.

"Sure. It's delicious, like always. I'm not making you late, am I?"

"No. Not at all. Let the bastards wait to play bridge. It isn't every Saturday I have my son for company. You know, one old lady who plays in our club has three kids and hasn't seen any of them in four years. Fuck bridge if it ever becomes that kind of a hang-up for me! Should I cancel on them?"

"I've got a piece to edit tonight, Pop. Just go enjoy yourself. I'd have myself closed away, anyway. Really."

Editing was easy, I found. That was, there were few changes I found I wanted to make. So I retyped the writing that night. It was finished as far as I was concerned. Fishbein might suggest—rather, demand—certain alterations, but I was satisfied and, yes, pleased.

As I reached the third floor landing of the Astoria apartment building, I heard a muffled rough staccato voice I recognized as Fishbein's. Did she have company? There were pauses and no answering voice. She was talking on the telephone. That was it! I decided not to interrupt her. Instead, I gazed out the hallway window, feeling as timorous as a college freshman about to hand in his first English essay to a renowned and tyrannical instructor, and angry with myself for such inner trepidation.

After a long silence, I concluded that the conversation was concluded, so I rapped on the door. Various chains jangled and bolts unthudded and, before releasing the last vestige of lock-smith art, she rasped, "That you, Chandler?"

"It is, indeed, you lucky woman."

"Bullshit!" she declared firmly. A sixtyish woman emerging from an adjacent apartment frowned in disapproval, but remained mute. Perhaps she had already engaged in a sparring match with her demonic Jewish-atheist neighbor or had the inherent prudence to avoid such a confrontation. I was snatched into the living room before I could speculate further.

"Do you have it?" she asked, unnecessarily really, since she snatched the folder containing the manuscript from my hand and went to the desk.

"Some greeting."

"You want I should give you a French kiss?"

"Something like that."

"Fuck you," she told me absently as she began to read.

"That's even better." She ignored me. The room was hot and blue with smoke. "Jesus, Fishbein! How can you stand it being this hot in here?"

A voice from afar said, "Is it? I've been working. I never pay attention to physical environments when I'm working. Open a window if you want. And shut up, I'm trying to concentrate."

I cranked out both old metal casement windows, hoping no one would call the fire department as the smoke billowed forth. Fishbein, being less than the perfect hostess, had withheld social niceties so I went to the kitchen and took a beer from the old, rumbling, once-white Amana refrigerator.

Fishbein was seated at the desk, frowning, in concentration I hoped, as she read. An unlit Camel was in her left hand and she twirled it absently. I studied her and wondered why I was so drawn to her. She was pretty in a careless, wild way and her body, regardless of her back, absolutely stupendous. But I had always avoided brash, foul-mouthed girls; no doubt my mother's influence. Was I trying to get even with my mother for something? If so, what was it? For not loving my father as much as I did? That was unfair. My mother had done her best to provide a stable home for me. In her own abstracted, subtle manner, she had been thoughtful and loving. Even her current subjects of harping, I could not totally dismiss. Yes, I probably should find some nice, polite girl and settle down and get a decent job. I could go to Manhattan tomorrow and walk along publishers' row and the chances were better than even I could, with my qualifications, land a job as a copyreader or rather, as they were beginning to call them, an editorial assistant. This would mean, after investing in suits and ties and shiny shoes and commuting a substantial distance in order to read usually boring submissions and be a whipping-boy for editors who made unwise decisions, earning approximately what I earned now standing behind the counter in jeans and a T-shirt laughing at Sammy's stale ribaldry. Mother, the CPA would understand all this and, no doubt, tacitly agree with the economics of this argument. But Mother, the mother would still be proud watching her necktied, be-suited son walking down the driveway to wait for a crosstown bus to catch that long, oozing pustule known as the subway, which in turn would vomit me into the bowels of Manhattan.

About the nice girl with whom I ought to settle down, that was altogether a different matter. My father had done that, to both my parents' ultimate regret, but he had waited until he was twenty-eight to make his error. Why couldn't I have another five years of casual bedding before settling down? Mother wouldn't understand that. There were no accountants' figures to rely upon. So, I could commit domestic hari-kari and she would not only accept it, but allow it to reinforce her opinion that men were foul creatures. Perhaps she was correct.

Gently closing the folder and pushing it away from her, Fishbein lit the Camel before looking at me and saying, "So, nobody was shitting me. You can write. This is good, Chandler; excellent, I'd say."

"Thanks. Now what?"

"We send it out to quality publications, what else? About time you started getting famous."

"It's really touching that you take such a close, personal interest in my career."

"Hold on, Chandler," she said sharply and, prodding herself in her cleavage, continued, "I am only interested in the career of one person. Number one. Me. You understand?"

"Altruism is rarely a driving emotion, especially, I would guess, in your case. So? Why do you care if I ever get anything published?"

She didn't answer immediately. Instead, she turned toward the window, took a final draw on her cigarette and, ignoring the overflowing ashtray, flicked the butt through the open window. I hoped no mother pushing a baby carriage was passing by on the sidewalk below. When she turned to face me she was smiling almost sweetly, but her voice was mocking. "You think you have me all figured out, don't you? That I'm a brazen opportunist. You don't know the first fucking thing about me, Chandler. Nothing. And you know something else? I don't think you want to know. If you knew what I know about me, it would scare you so much you'd grab this folder and take the stairs two at a time and bypass the car because it would be symbolic of me. Then you would get a city bus and run home to mommy on City Island!" Her voice had become shrill; the smile had vanished.

"Try me. Tell me something about you. See if I run away."

"No, Chandler, I won't."

"Why not?"

She looked down at the sculptured tan rug and appeared to be studying the six or seven burned spots in it; either counting them or perhaps noticing their presence for the first time. Then, in a low voice, "Either you're more stupid than I guessed or I'm a better actress than I thought."

"What in hell is that supposed to mean?"

"You honestly don't know, do you? You complete asshole. I've been trying to nail you for the past year, and desperately afraid I would. I'd...think back, Chandler. Think! Me always around you, trying to make you notice. Hell, I even offered to pick you up, all the way up on fucking City Island." She paused for breath.

Then it flashed in my mind; little light bulbs of recollection flooded every little chunk of gray matter. I saw Fishbein always seated next to me in class. Fishbein constantly asking me questions. Fishbein hailing me, only me, across a crowded hallway.

And Fishbein offering what I thought to be car-pooling, but was in reality chauffeuring service. Yes, I now understood that peculiar pull joined in a conflict of repulsion. But I didn't know *why*.

"When I saw you on that bench on Willis Avenue, I came this close to fainting." She held out two ink-marked fingers. "I'd really given up. I was relieved, finally, but it still hurt like hell. But there you were, sitting like a derelict and all of the old longing and all the fear came back to me. And now I'm scared shitless, but it's worse because you're right here! Do you understand what I'm telling you?!"

"I guess. That you like me but you don't want to get involved. Shit, I can live with that. Why make such a big deal out of it?"

"It goes way deeper than that, but that's enough for a satisfactory working relationship."

Never before had a woman screamed at me, but one was about to. I realized it even as I spoke the two simple inane sentences—actually one sentence and one fragment—which caused it. I said: "What are we going to work on? Making a baby?"

She stood abruptly and her dark eyes fixed a scorching light on me. Then she screamed, "Don't you ever say that to me! You filthy son-of-a-bitch! Never say that! Do you hear?"

For some reason I wasn't scared; I just wished I hadn't opened the windows. "Sure," I said, stepping past her and picking up my folder, "I'm sure all Astoria heard you. And don't worry about my saying that again, or anything else. Go screw yourself, Fishbein." I opened the door to the hall and added, "And you're right about one thing. I'm taking the bus home."

At the landing between the third and second floors I heard her say, "Chandler?" My impulse was to keep walking but I paused without turning or speaking.

"Chandler. Turn around."

I did. She was standing at the head of the stairway. My God! Fishbein had tears in her eyes! Running down her cheeks!

"Yes," she said quietly, reading my mind, "That's right. Tears. Now you've seen two things that no one else has ever seen before, my back and my tears." I started to turn again but she continued speaking. "Now you're going to see a third thing no one has ever seen before. Fishbein pleading. Please come back, Chandler. Please." I obeyed.

"Since you obviously didn't like my last conjecture, suppose you just tell me what it is you want us to work on." I had reseated myself on the sofa.

She came over and knelt down facing me, taking both my hands in hers. "Please listen. I'm sorry, but you've got to understand, I can't ever have a baby. Never."

"How was I to know? How do you know? Have you tried?"

"That isn't what I mean." She held our arms apart. "Look at this body. I'd guess it is very fertile. Look at these hips. I suspect I could deliver an eight-pounder single-handed without a whimper of pain. What I'm telling you is I could never stand to bring a baby into the world."

"Why not? The world isn't perfect, but it's got some good things going for it."

She held my hands to her face, her elbows resting on my knees. "I'd be afraid, Chandler, afraid that I've inherited my old lady's craziness. You see, I might start beating my child, thinking I was getting even for what was done to me. I couldn't stand that. Do you understand?"

"I guess so. There is such a thing as an abortion. They're quite legal now."

"No! I am the ultimate liberated woman, but one part of the menu I have no part in is abortions. That's beating a baby before it's even *born*, for christsake. No one can change my mind about that subject. At least I had some good times as well as the shitty ones when I was little."

"Does that mean you're actually a virgin? I haven't seen one of those since I was in the sixth grade."

"No. I was brought up on the streets of Brooklyn and knew I could do as I pleased until I had a period. Some high school senior screwed me for nearly a year. The greasy wop told me we were going steady. That he was in love with me." She gave a short mirthless laugh. "He didn't know I didn't care. A dick was a dick. Then I found out that, to him, a cunt was a cunt, because I went down to the basement one day, where all the tenants had storage lockers, and there was this dago with my sister, her lying up on a table. She was buck naked with her little points just shaking away while he banged the hell out of her. I wanted to laugh, but I waited until I was upstairs. Rhoda's ugly now, but she was worse when she was eleven. Just fat and flab, and a hole. I figured the guy was really just doing the equivalent of jerking-off. Next time he came close and asked for a piece, I told him to fuck off. A month later I started a period and that was that. So over eleven years of abstinence since."

"Did your mother beat your sister, too?" I asked suddenly, curious.

"No. Of course not. Rhoda was ugly and I was pretty. That was what got to her crazy thinking. And yes, I'll admit it, that is mainly why I can't stand her. The old lady would yell, 'Sure! You'll be a Rockette or do Broadway, like I could have done, hadna' been for lousy children ruining my career! You and your father! But you were first! Wrecked my life!' Then she would beat the shit out of me. Once, literally. I passed out and shit on the living room rug. She beat me for that, too. Sure, I could have been a Rockette if I didn't have to turn my back on the audience."

"Where was your father while all this was happening?"

"On the road. He was a salesman, a drummer, a peddler,

whatever you want to call it, for a wholesale garment company. When my old lady killed herself, they were good to him. Gave him a desk job so he could be home every night. It ruined him. He loved to travel. Then with the new job he came home every night, but it was to drink himself senseless. Later, when Rhoda and I were older, they gave him his old territory back. He was happy, drank less, but it was too late. Probably he had cancer then, but he worked on between treatments until the end. Died in a motel room in Fall River, Massachusetts. Amen."

I felt terrible, so I said with false joviality, "Well, we still have a date tonight. Remember?"

"I do. What time are we to get there?"

"Seven-thirty."

"What should I wear?"

"I don't know. A dress, maybe?" I suggested tentatively.

Fishbein laughed raucously. "We need nourishment first. And a beer." She released my hands and went to the kitchen calling over her shoulder, "You don't believe I own a dress, do you?"

I didn't know for sure but not wanting to say no or yes, I countered, "How should I know? I've never seen you in anything but jeans and usually a leather jacket."

I followed her into the kitchen, where she was opening two cans of Franco-American spaghetti. "We're going to eat Italian tonight, Chandler," she informed me with flat sarcasm. Then she handed me a bottle of beer from the refrigerator. "I might surprise you. Even pantyhose I've got."

Seated at the dinette table, our pasta feast concluded, Fishbein asked suddenly, "Is the car all right? Did you have trouble?"

"Not a bit. The old clunker runs better than it looks. Why?"

"Think about it, Chandler," she said darkly. "Our mode of transportation will seriously impact what I choose from my vast wardrobe."

I shrugged. "If it went round-trip to Mineola, it should get us to Kew Gardens and back, and, I hope, to City Island."

"You're going back? Tonight?" She said "back" like I was returning to Louie DeJerolamo's repair shop to bed down.

"I'd planned to."

"That's dumb as hell. Just stay here. It would be closer for you to go to work in the morning."

"I'm afraid Mother would feel...I believe alienated is the word."

"Fuck her. Be practical."

"Look, Fishbein, I'm not a 'mommy's boy,' but I don't have any hideous memories of my mother. Boring, maybe, but she does provide food and shelter. And then..."

"And then," Fishbein interrupted, "she is assuming her darling son is screwing the brains out of what she has summed up as the trashy Brooklyn girl to whom she has taken already an instinctive dislike."

"You think she did? Not like you?"

"Think? Shit, the noble parlor on City Island was magically transported to the North Pole the very second I was ushered in."

"Mother tends to be a bit aloof to anyone at first."

"Don't shit me, Chandler. I can detect genuine loathing when I see it. Me—the coarse Jew-woman."

"Did she say that?"

"Of course not. She didn't need to."

"It's possible you imagined it."

"It's possible I'm enjoying an all-enveloping orgasm as we speak. Look, I've got to get ready. You want a beer, get it. If you are interested in reading poetry, look on the desk in a brown envelope. I got my first rejection back today. Poetry is hard to sell. I warn you, Chandler, a lot of them are about you."

Only her last comment, before she left the room to engage in all the noisily erratic activities of a woman readying herself for an evening out, piqued my curiosity enough to begin reading. Poetry was lost on me. As an artistic medium, I had been taught that it had value, insouciance, but I simply didn't appreciate it. Especially blank verse which, to me, were just powdery wisps of thoughts and hidden meanings. Nevertheless Fishbein had offered, really commanded, so I began reading. That was unfair. She just had an imperious tone of voice. The manuscript was entitled *Street Smart* and the gist of the collection was an allegorical journey through the New York streets. But there weren't the unclear nuances present which I associated, and hence disliked, in most other modern poetry. This was clear and vibrant, even strident, writing.

But as I read on I could see no reference to me either by name or in symbolism or abstraction. Then I read the passage:

> *There is my love across a crowded hallway*
> *A corridor inadequately cleaned too often*
> *Will I approach him?*
> *Can I touch him?*
> *Is he real?*
> *Yes, for now he laughs*
> *But am I allowed to love?*
> *I am terrified to love*
> *For to love is to destroy*
> *Silent good night for a hundredth time*

Was that about me? Once before, only once, I had thought I was in love, but I had not been terrified and certainly had not felt destructive. That affair of five years' past had not been in my thoughts until now. Really, I hadn't been heartbroken when the romance ended. I recalled that idyllic summer of 1970. I had just graduated from high school, had my scholarship to Fordham and, with Mother's grudging permission, I was spending the summer out in Mineola. Then, when Pop drove me to his house, there at the curb was the shiny, almost new VW resplendent in British racing green and he had pointed, handed me the keys and simply said, "Congratulations, Roy."

On my very first trip to the park of my childhood—this time in my exquisite new second-hand car—I encountered not Charlotte, my romantic entrapper, but beautiful Christine Arthur in a revealing green and yellow halter, scant white shorts and no shoes; a living Barbie doll but with all the tempting orifices in place. Christine was spending the summer with her grandfather, one Sidney Arthur, who had been the developer of the neighborhood and who, in fact, had named Arthur Avenue, although I've never had the heart to tell this last to my father. If you're reading this now, Pop, relaxing in retirement in Uncle Manny's guest house, overlooking the Loxahatchee River in North Palm Beach, now you know.

Anyway, the first night the halter top came away without protest. The next night the shorts and panties and by the third evening we began a routine of joyous regular copulation, only halted by one four-day hiatus due to nature taking its course with Christine. That was strange because, as I sat in Gladys Fishbein's shabby apartment, the only remark of Christine's I could remember was, "It's usually five days. My body must be anxious to get back in action."

I had been, for we found all manner of ways to fuck in accommodation of the definite givens of the interior of a Volkswagen. It was possible that some of the wear to the king-pins began during that first season of my ownership.

As that summer waned we had no less sexual appetite, but conversely jointly knew but never stated the finiteness of the interlude. By the time I returned to City Island we were both pleased that Christine had not been impregnated, I had contracted no social disease, our bruises and scrapes resultant of automotive lustful antics would heal and that neither of us would ever write to each other although we promised faithfully to do so. All of which was far superior to the disconcerting demand of the Charlotte of my childhood that, in addition to kissing her, I was also required to rub the two hard, bulging lumps on her chest.

I had given up all pretext of reading, and was staring at the disordered desk in the corner. It was silent and warm in the room. A rough voice floated over to me. "Chandler?" A pause as I focused. Then: "What do you think?"

I gazed at the female strength and mobility confronting me. It was awesome in its utter understatement. The clothing I drank in first. That was the easy part. A white oxford-cloth blouse, because of the lack of darts and her ample breasts, split ever so slightly revealing a hint of lace bra and cleavage. Then a knee-length navy skirt with a side slit, hose and heeled blue sandals. Her hair, brushed so much some curls had taken on copper tones in the sunset light, had a straight, severe part in the center. The subtle foundation make-up was overwhelmed by mascara which made her eyes appear coal black. Traces of pink blush on her cheekbones and matching lipstick at once tempered, yet exemplified, her features. My only criticism was an over-abundant application of blue eye shadow. Unquestionably, Fishbein was voluptuous, powerful Jewish-atheist womanhood at its finest. "My God!" I breathed, "I don't believe it."

"Not bad, huh?" She clicked her tongue in her cheek and winked simultaneously as only a true New York woman can do instinctively, but no one from anywhere else can fake. She took a cigarette from the pack in her blue handbag and lit it.

Just then I was unreasoningly compelled to get up from the sofa and cross the room and kiss her, all three of which I did. To my surprise, she was most yielding, her lips soft, and when I drew away she didn't yell or look angry, or sad or startled. She just asked quietly, "Why did you do that?"

"Just because I wanted to."

She smiled and admonished mildly, "Well, don't do it again for awhile. I don't want my make-up messy; what did you think of it?"

"Very tender. Just…"

"The manuscript, Chandler," she said scathingly. "I don't know any way to describe a kiss, for christsake."

I could, I thought, describe a kiss in prolonged paragraph length, written or oral, replete with adjectives and verbs, but I just said, "It's more strident and powerful than any of the verse I've read over the years to become convinced that poetry sucks. Why do you like it so much?"

"What I write is really spare prose. It's almost a mathematical exercise to me. Not including one extra spare word I think is a challenge." She added cryptically, "Like you are a challenge. Let's go."

The evening with Zuma Alcorn got off to an uncertain start. Fishbein had already knocked on the front door of the newish, brick-front, semi-detached dwelling with its large window box filled with flourishing geraniums. Zuma opened the door while I was still locking the car, saw an unfamiliar young woman and a strange car in her driveway, but didn't see me. Thus, she thought the young woman was pandering for a break in the theater and as I approached, she was telling a protesting Fishbein, "See, honey, the best I can do is give you my card with a recommendation note. I must say you've got the build and the looks to dance the line, but it's a lousy way to start. Anyway, you show my card to Bill Upjohn, he's the casting…"

Seeing me, she broke off and issued one of her belly-laughs. "Why, you two are together! You picked out a beauty, here, Roy. Introduce us."

"This is Gladys Fishbein and, of course, Zuma Alcorn needs no introduction. My colleague has a habit of staying about five or ten steps ahead of me mentally and physically with some unusual results, as you've just seen."

"Well, never mind. Come in! Roy has spent the past six months keeping my mind agile; making me remember things I was certain I'd forgotten or never known."

"And I'm making him write it down," Fishbein interjected, handing her the folder I didn't realize she had brought along.

"Good for you! Much as I've enjoyed Roy's charming company, I was beginning to think nothing concrete was ever going to come of it. May I?"

"Most definitely," Fishbein said, giving me a bland smile and studying her surroundings intently.

As she read, several times she chuckled, once she frowned and finishing, she handed the folder back to Fishbein, smiled at me and said simply, "It's all there. Give me a cigarette, please."

I put my pack on the table and she lit one greedily. With obvious relief Gladys lit a Camel and asked, "Are you trying to quit?"

"No, but I smoke as little as possible when I'm working. It makes the timbre of the voice erratic and the musicians have to adjust to it. Back in the old days, that didn't matter, all of us kept bottles in our dressing rooms. A few belts before the performance and the voice was perfect again. God! No wonder so many of us died so young!"

She was silent a moment, then asked, "Where did you get that information about my doing troop entertaining during World War II? I don't remember mentioning that."

"You didn't. I was going to ask you why you hadn't told me about it."

"Ah! There is a reason for that. Just after my divorce ended ten years of misery for both Jackie Gould and yours truly, a marriage we both desperately wanted to make work and it wouldn't, I fell hopelessly in love, in just one afternoon, with a handsome young army sergeant barely half my age. Oh, nothing happened between us and I never saw him again. But it made me certain my emotions were all fouled up and I was determined never to marry again. As you know, I never did." She paused to grind out her cigarette.

"I see," I said, not seeing at all. Zuma had shared far more intimate anecdotes than this.

"Do you know who the soldier was?" she asked.

"No, of course not."

"U.S. Army Staff Sergeant Arthur Chandler."

"Pop? I'll be damned. Just this weekend he mentioned, when I told him who I was writing about, that he had once meet you. When he was stationed in Georgia."

Gladys shifted in her armchair. "You have a very lovely home, but one thing seems strange."

"What's that, dear?"

"I would have assumed that there would be pictures and mementos all over the place, I mean with a career like yours."

"Oh, I have them all. Packed away in drawers and boxes and more in a trunk in the basement. But so many of the memories are sad and the pictures show me at twenty-five and thirty-five and then I go to the mirror and see a seventy-five-year-old woman. No thanks. I'm grateful for all that past, but I don't want it on display. Besides, I'm too damned honest. If I put out the accolades and glamorous pictures, I'd feel obliged to have my two divorce decrees and the bills for past due taxes on my farm framed and on display.

"But I'm being a dreadful hostess. What will you have to drink, Gladys? I want a good, stiff Scotch and water."

"Just a beer, if you have it. I'm like Chandler."

"Is that what you call him? I like that." She laughed and turned to me, "Come on, Chandler, get your own damned beer. I haven't got three hands."

"You're a bad influence on this gracious lady, Fishbein," I called over my shoulder as I followed Zuma to the kitchen.

"That is an intense and, I suspect, brilliant young woman you have out there, Roy. Do you know it?"

"She made me write what you just read. I did it in one day and here I've been procrastinating for six months. She scares me a little and Mother took an immediate dislike to her."

Zuma laughed. "She isn't the type mothers would take to

and her being so beautiful, which I don't have to remind you of, doesn't help either."

"She *is* beautiful. I went to graduate school with her for over a year and never noticed. Of course, usually she was wearing a motorcycle helmet and a leather jacket so it was hard..."

A peal of laughter. "A helmet! God! Does she ride a motorcycle, too?"

"Of course. All over the city."

"Lord, Roy! You have got a wild one. Think you can handle her?"

"I guess I'll find out."

Settled with our drinks, Zuma lit another of my cigarettes and tapped the folder, "So you two don't think there is enough for an entire book. I didn't in the first place." She didn't sound at all miffed.

"There is plenty for a book," Fishbein assured her, "but we want to get Chandler here a super writing credit; make him an authority in the field. Then we begin our collaborative project I've been telling about."

"You haven't told *me*, Fishbein," I said irritably. "Every time I ask you, some scene develops."

"That's your fault. If you'll listen I will tell you the plan, Chandler, right down to the last minute fucking detail." I glanced over to where Zuma was shaking in silent mirth. "All right, already. Listen. I didn't have this nailed down in my mind until I read what you have written. It's good. Superb, in fact. And in reading it, the title of our book even came to me."

"A book?"

"Yes, a book. Basically it will be a collection of the century's greatest women singers and actresses. Each chapter will be a biographical essay on a famous woman in the field. It will not only trace their careers but tell most importantly what happened to each of them. Dead or alive. See? And I grabbed the title from what you wrote about Zuma Alcorn saying that when she was down on her luck, the song 'Three Little Words' turned into 'Go to hell!'

"The title is going to be *Three Little Words*. You see!? It's perfect! We'll find a song title of three words for each performer, a song with which each is closely associated."

"Suppose, just suppose, you two can't find a song of three words to match each woman? What then?" Zuma was warming to the project. I could tell.

"Yeah, Fishbein. What then?"

"We certainly won't exclude anyone we want to profile because we can't, but I'm almost certain we can link almost anyone to some three-word song title. I've done research on song titles. A majority have three words."

"Where do I come in?" I asked.

"You write it, asshole."

"What will you be doing meanwhile?"

"Listen, Chandler, I'm going to do all the research. I'm good at that. I'm good at poetry, or at least I think I am, but I'm a lousy prose writer; I admit it. You write from my research. It's simple. In fact, you've got the easy job."

"Exactly where do I come in?" Zuma inquired. "I'm an old woman. All of what I've told Chandler, I believe is correct, but I wouldn't bet a lawsuit on it." They were beginning to sound alike.

Fishbein shook her head violently. "No, no. Your capacity is strictly advisory. You will receive acknowledgment but no liability. What's important is that you read over the material for glaring errors or items and anecdotes we ought to include."

"Wait a second, Fishbein. Tell me who we include and who we bypass. We're talking hundreds of performers."

"You and I will hash that out while we work." She spoke negligently, but I saw it as a genuine source of conflict which she did not choose to address just then.

"Jesus, Fishbein! Why didn't you leave some fucking windows open! This place is uninhabitable."

"Fuck yourself! Want to search around for Ralph the rapist every night? Not me."

"This is the third floor. Ralph is not an accomplished wall-climber to my knowledge."

"Just call your mother and shut up. You expect air-conditioning already? At a free motel?" A whirl of white crossed my vision which I assumed were my sheet and pillow. They plopped down neatly on the sofa.

I went to the sweltering kitchen and dialed Mother's number. She picked up on the first ring which meant she was either in bed watching television or in the kitchen drinking her nightcap cup of tea. "Hi, Mother. It's your wandering son."

"Where are you?" she asked, her tone suggesting that she knew damn well precisely where I was.

"Over in Astoria. I am going to stay here again tonight. I'll be home after work tomorrow."

"I see. I appreciate your calling to tell me." The telephone receiver I gripped was suddenly seven degrees below zero, unlike the ninety degrees of everything else in the apartment. To avoid frostbite I returned it to its cradle. In the living room, I cranked the windows out to their maximum openness, then spread the sheet upon the sofa. Fishbein's room was dark and silent; apparently closed for the night.

"Sweet dreams, collaborator," I called softly and turned off the light, collapsing onto the sofa. This was July...something. Five years ago tonight I'd fucked Christine Arthur thirty-nine times and gotten one blow-job as a bonus. I hadn't been celibate since—nor before, for that matter—but this relationship with Fishbein clearly boded no sexual pleasure.

Writing must be more emotionally taxing than I'd thought. Quickly, I began to fall into slumber, when I heard the words, "Jews never go to heaven."

"What?" Suddenly I was very awake—or was I dreaming?

"That's what my old man used to say when he'd come in after a bad week on the road. He said it at my mother's funeral. I'm saying it now."

"I don't understand."

"Just that I am lying here naked, my cunt filled with a foam, which the label on the can insists, will heartlessly murder every one of the thousands of sperm attackers you pump into me before they can assault the first precious egg. My crotch feels like the Columbia River in salmon spawning season. So come on and fuck me, Chandler, assuming you put on the condom that no male pig leaves out of his wallet in anticipation of an imagined desirous pussy."

"Sorry, Fishbein. I don't have one. Besides, your offer is about as tempting as a fistful of warm vegetable oil. I could just as easily jack off. In fact, I might. One of the stains on this couch looks like someone already has. Forget it!"

A few sounds from the bedroom suggested that she might be crying. It was possible but I just slept. I didn't masturbate either. But she repeated just once, "Jews never go to heaven."

*****

I awoke to a stiff, crinkly, uncomfortable feeling around my genitals. Oh, no! Surely I hadn't...I reached down gingerly into my briefs. To my immediate relief then subsequent embarrassment, I drew out a folded sheet of typing paper. I sat up and lit a cigarette. The apartment was silent and stifling. Unfolding the paper, I read:

Coffee is on. Don't forget to turn it off!
Bread & jelly are in refrigerator. Toaster on counter.
Had to go downtown early. Call me.
— *F.*

P.S. At 7:02 A.M. you had a monster erection.

I smiled, padded to the kitchen, poured coffee and turned off the brewer as instructed. We New Yorkers always meant Manhattan when we used the term "downtown." I pictured her roaring down FDR Drive on the Harley, bent forward in anticipation and determination.

*****

"Jesus!" Sammy Shinbaum greeted me, "you look like ya spent the night on a park bench in Harlem."

"Thanks, Sammy, but it was a sofa in Astoria."

"Some girl wouldn't give ya no pussy?"

"That's about it."

"Ditch her," he advised. "You a good lookin' young stud. Pussies galore out there to be had for the askin'."

"What looks so bad about me anyway?"

He studied me a moment. "Can't put my finguh on it. You could use a shave, though."

"You want me to go home and shave?"

"Hell, no. Halfa my customahs need a shave." He laughed. "The wimmen too! Listen to this, Roy. See, there is this goy and he wants he should be a Jew. So he goes to the rabbi and the rabbi first thing asks him to take out his dick. Well…" The telephone rang, saving me from hearing the long, threadbare monologue related to circumcision.

Old Mrs. Horowitz strode into the store to buy her weekly lamb roast. There was a well established ritual to her Monday morning shopping. "Good morning, Mrs. Horowitz," it began.

"Good morning, Roy. Are you still working in this dreadful place?" it continued. "And you with such a fine education. Where is that detestable proprietor?"

The toilet flushed on cue and Sammy appeared buckling his belt. "I'm through shittin', Roy." Mock surprise. "Oh, Mrs. Horowitz. Fine day, ain't it?"

"Samuel Shinbaum! Watch your language and your English. For forty-one years I taught English and I am constantly exposed to one of my failures. Now, wash your hands before you cut my roast."

"Yes, Mrs. Horowitz," he replied humbly, not washing his hands, going to the back room for the piece of meat he had cut an hour ago, and reappearing carrying it gently as though it were an ostrich egg.

"That's no six-pound roast," she objected as always.

"It's really six poun' three, but I only charge you for six."

"Roy, you weigh it on this scale. Sammy has a heavy thumb." She scrutinized the meter. "Aha! Just six pounds and one!"

"Well, gimmie a break. I don't see so good early in the mawnin'."

"Well, not good, Samuel."

I wrapped the roast and handed it to her. Like most of the regular customers, Mrs. Horowitz had a charge account. "I hope you enjoy it," I told her.

"See what fine manners Roy has, Samuel?"

"Yeah, Mrs. Horowitz. Have a nice day."

"Don't say 'nice.' That word means stupid. You want me to have a stupid day? Well, I've already had a stupid day by coming into this store! Goodbye Roy, Samuel." The ritual was concluded.

*****

Mother was seated in an armchair on the sun porch reading the financial section of the *Times*. She glanced up when I came in the back door. "Don't slam that door, Roy!" she said sharply. "One of the panes is loose. I'd like for you to get some putty this weekend and repair it."

"Sure. Is that any way to welcome your long lost son?"

She smiled briefly and I kissed her cheek. "Your absence was your choice, you know."

I nodded. "I know, but have I changed?" I gripped her forearms and looked dramatic. "Do I look any older? Tell me!"

She laughed and swatted away my hands, one at a time. "You always have been able to make me laugh." The smile faded and she made the obligatory, disinterested inquiry, "How is your father?"

"Just fine. He's had the house completely remodeled and bought a new green Lincoln."

"I'm glad he's doing so well."

"He just said he could afford it now that the house is paid for and he doesn't have a son in college any more."

"Humph! He didn't mention that his son got to live scot-free all the time that son was in college."

"Cut the crap, Mother! You know as well as I do that he paid you child support for years after he was either legally or even morally required to. Until three months ago!"

My mother looked like she was about to cry. Frequently she gave that look, but I had never actually seen her weep. Now she said sorrowfully, "That's why I hate for you to go to your father's! He always poisons you against me!"

"*You're* the one who brought up the subject! *He* never mentioned it!"

She shrugged and resumed her reading.

Deciding it might be fun to goad her further, I asked casually, "How do you like my new girlfriend?"

"The Goldfine girl? She's Jewish, isn't she?"

"Fishbein." I corrected, adding, "No, she's an atheist."

"Oh. She seemed a little too...uh...flamboyant."

"Very definitely."

"Is that whom you've been sleeping with?" Then, flatly, "Is she good in bed?"

"Screws like a rabbit."

"That's disgusting, Roy!"

"You asked. Truth of the matter is, I have no idea. I slept on the sofa both nights, which you can believe or not as you see fit."

Mother looked back at the Stock Exchange listings and said absently, "You're a man now. Those are your own decisions." Then she brightened. "Oh, by the way, Sally Becker is coming home his weekend. You always like to see her."

"Is she?" Well, that would be a soothing interlude from the unfathomable, complex Fishbein. I knew, as my mother could not, that beneath the demure, mousy-haired, wholesome facade of Sally Becker lurked a totally sensual creature with the sexual habits of the proverbial alley cat. It was to Sally whom I surrendered my virginity when I was fifteen. In the Becker's basement playroom, I had fumblingly gotten my pants down while she, already naked, had urged, "Come on! Hurry!"

As I mounted her, she rose up too far. I almost nailed the wrong hole. She admonished me, whispering venomously, "Not there! I'm not into doing Greek." Then, parting the sparse brown hair of the experienced opening, I thrust into her, managing to pound stroke after stroke into her despite the fact that I climaxed after the third or fourth drive. "I'll look forward to seeing her," I told my mother simply. This would be an uncomplicated piece of ass. Sally, I mean.

"What's on the menu, tonight?" I asked.

"I'm trying a new recipe for curried chicken."

"Sounds interesting," I said, groaning inwardly, and plucked a beer from the refrigerator.

Mother laughed shortly. "Interesting, huh? You're not sticking your neck out, are you?"

"Nope. That's where the chicken made *its* mistake. I'm going to go take a shower."

"You need to shave, too."

"So I've been told, but I am going to wait until in the morning for that, unless I really offend you."

She shook her head, absorbed in the paper. "I don't care."

"Guess what?"

"Hmm?"

"Pop offered to let me move in with him."

She frowned. "That would be a long commute to Melrose Avenue."

"That's what I told him. But if I take a job downtown it will be a straight shot on the train."

"Really?" Mother's interest was drawn away from the stock market. "Do you have an offer?"

"Well, no. But male prostitutes are in big demand in Greenwich Village. The fags prefer them to be eighteen or, better yet, sixteen, but I'm not over the hill yet, and I've been told that my endowments…"

"Roy! That's horrible!"

"I got your attention!" I laughed and ran upstairs.

Beyond an almost regimentally applied schedule of maintenance of periodic painting and replacement of outdated plumbing and structural and electrical components, Mother had only made one notable improvement in her house since her parents had commissioned it to be built in the mid 1930s. That feature was a generous stall shower in the upstairs bathroom. A large utility closet had been appropriated for this purpose but, since there was already a linen closet, its absence went unnoticed.

This conversion had coincided roughly with my fourteenth birthday, and vastly accommodated comfortable masturbation, letting the jets of hot water play upon my genitals until self-gratification was realized. Certainly Mother had not created this sensual womb to relieve me of the freezing temptations of the basement, but it was nevertheless welcomed.

Self-abuse was not on my pondering agenda that Monday night as I adjusted the taps, snapped closed the door to the compartment behind me and enveloped myself, in fact became a part of, the hot, fragrant, moist, fetid environment. Since Mother's installation of the unit and to this day I have remained an avid "shower thinker." This, my mother warned me early on, had a marked effect on the fuel bills and I have since often upbraided myself for the astronomical utility bills the practice causes. So I thought; deeply, enquiringly.

On Sunday at around seven o'clock in the evening, I had kissed Gladys Fishbein. It had not been a sloppy, mutual tongue-lashing kiss, but it had the effect of sucking my guts out and making me feel giddy and out of control. This meant I might have a degree of romantic interest in her. So what? She had made it quite clear that she had had, unbeknown to me, considerable desire for me, but she had no idea how to pursue it or whether, in fact, she wanted to. But why not? Why did she admit, both verbally and in her writing, that she had a destructive nature? I was fairly strong emotionally, I thought. So what could she do to me? If she broke off the affair, so what? I wouldn't have very many regrets. Fishbein had made but one angry offering akin to that which a necrophiliac might enjoy.

On the other hand, next weekend I would enjoy the moral slackness of Sally Becker which offered, depending upon her sexual appetite of the moment, two or three or four non-obligatory pieces of ass. For that, I could be a stalwart aggressor.

What, if she knew or found out, would be Fishbein's reaction to such casual sex? Was she jealous, or did she even care? I did not know. What I did know was that she was essentially unknown to me. Possibly unknowable.

The shower shifted gears meaning the furnace was switching to its auxiliary tank. Time in the shower incubus was limited. Both my parents had extreme misgivings about my involvement with Fishbein, although Pop had not yet met her. My father's reservations stemmed from a preconception that this was a strong woman. Mother, in her own way, had been a strong woman, so it was possible that he just had an understandable aversion to strength in women. But in 1975, weak females, except for those of Sally Becker's stripe, had become a scarce commodity. Then it occurred to me that I was trying to play to an audience of markedly varied tastes. Therefore I would, I resolved, perform only for my own benefit. I snapped the shower controls off. Fuck everyone.

*****

On Wednesday night, I took the telephone receiver from my mother's proffering hand, her nostrils flared in distaste and eyes critical, suggesting it was Fishbein, whom in fact it was. "Hey, you human turd. Am I not entitled to a simple phone call already?"

"Haven't had any provocative thoughts to pass along. No one has stolen your car, if that's any comfort."

"Fuck the car. You could have just called to talk to me." She sounded plaintive.

"Sorry. I should have."

"And your old lady is listening to every word you say."

"That's right."

"What you got planned this weekend?"

"My mother has me socially obligated."

A pause. "How about Sunday night? I've got some research ready for you to start writing about."

"I can arrange that. Everything going OK with you?"

Quietly, "Yeah." Then, "I miss you, Chandler." The connection was severed.

"Goodbye," I told the dial tone.

It was surprising how little I knew about Sally Becker's family. After all, when we were horny teenagers attempting to screw one another to oblivion, it would have seemed inappropriate to inquire about genealogy. Between couplings, however, she had once informed me that she had a much older half-brother, Bert, resulting from her mother's failed first marriage. She also had once said that when she was ten, and Bert was about to leave for college, as a going away present he had torn away her maidenhead. The event had been recounted to me as though she had never experienced remorse or regret, nor even offered resistance. Perhaps she was a born tart.

In any case, when she called me late Friday afternoon, inviting me to visit for the evening, I promptly went to the drugstore and purchased six stout-appearing condoms. I was taking no chances on the inconvenience of a social disease. During her career at the University of Connecticut, where she had majored in art and sexual intercourse—not necessarily in that order—a mutual friend, Carol Abrams, had told me Sally had had two abortions.

As I walked along the sidewalk, I was reminded that I had ties here at City Island that I had been taking for granted. Friends, too. Carol had been my date to the senior prom. We still wrote to one another since her graduation from college and subsequent relocation to Albany where she was employed by the state in the department promoting tourism. My neighborhood always had a faint odor of salt air and a maritime atmosphere. I was just abreast of Carol's family home. It had a porthole in the front door flanked by two small brass mermaids.

The Beckers were relative newcomers to the community. It seemed to me they had moved here about ten years previously from somewhere in Connecticut. Mr. Otto Becker was a warehouse foreman with a huge importer of wicker junk located in Brooklyn and her mother was quite an accomplished painter, selling through one of Manhattan's better galleries. No doubt this had influenced Sally to be an art major and, no, I have no idea about Mrs. Orris Becker's moral standards.

Number 14 Jonquil Court was a near clone to Mother's house. The only difference, and that was not visible from the street, was that the stairway to the basement was inside and much of that chamber had been fashioned into a tile floored, knotty-pine paneled recreation room in stark contrast to Mother's basement featuring an oil burner, a broken couch, and age-stained, sperm-stiffened rags and newspapers of yesteryear. My mother's excessive tidiness did not encompass her cellar—except to the extent that she asked on occasion, "Have you cleaned the basement lately?" I would always give an affirmative response, which alone satisfied her.

Any misgivings that a college degreed Sally Becker might have reassessed her values were immediately dispelled when she answered the doorbell and, giving her cheerleader leap, embraced me while worming her tongue deep into my mouth. It was her fake cheerleader ways that drew my mother and presumably her parents into the erroneous belief that she was wholesome rather than the complete strumpet that, in fact, she was.

This is not to say she was an unattractive young woman. Her blue eyes were clear and playful, although the lashes were sparse. She had a short, turned-up nose, a generous mouth and slightly thick neck, all of which were enhanced by springy pale brown hair and a pink healthy complexion, creating the cheerleader image. She had never served in that capacity except on a one-to-one basis during which she bounced up and down a great deal and chants of "Harder! Harder!" and "I'm coming! I'm coming!" were panted avidly.

Mr. and Mrs. Becker were in the living room, both standing, he shrugging into a suit jacket while she made final adjustments to her make-up, peering closely into a wall mirror. As Sally led me by the hand into the room, Orris Becker turned and smiled brightly. "Why, hello, Roy! So nice to see you! How is your mother?"

"Just fine, thank you."

"How is your father?" Otto Becker chimed in.

"He's fine, too. I just spent last weekend with him."

"Roy, I hope you won't think we're rude, but we have been waiting ages for these tickets. We're going to dine downtown beforehand and probably have a nightcap after. Sally's going to cook for you."

To cover up odd, outward manifestations that I was calculating how many times I would be able to fuck their daughter, I said, "I'm sure she is a good cook. What show are you seeing?"

The Ultimate Rainbow. It stars an old timer who's making a comeback, Zuma Alcorn. I saw it—goodness! —when I was younger than Sally. You've probably never heard of her."

"Yes. I've seen the show." I didn't bother to add that I hadn't waited ages because I had been given a complimentary ticket. "As a matter of fact, I just finished writing a biographical essay about Zuma Alcorn."

"How interesting!" she exclaimed with disinterest. "Come on, Otto. We'll be late," she said to her husband who was waiting impatiently by the door.

"So," I said to Sally, "how does it feel to be a college graduate?"

"It feels unemployed."

"I know the feeling. Any leads?"

She led the way back to the kitchen, shaking her head. "Nothing so far. Not anything that sounded interesting. How about you?"

"Sammy Shinbaum's Kosher Meat Market."

"Do you think we're unemployable?" Sally handed me a beer and then mixed a Canadian Club and ginger ale for herself.

"I guess we could be teachers."

"Fuck that! Mom has made an appointment for me Monday morning for an interview with an ad agency. It might offer something worth considering."

"I hope so."

Sally raised her glass in toast. "To lustful encounters."

"I can always drink to that." I swallowed beer. "What are you cooking?"

"Oysters Rockefeller. Oysters are rumored to be an aphrodisiac."

"So I've heard. Have I ever needed one before? You sure as hell haven't."

She studied me. "I still don't. Come on." Sally could sound and seem seductive even when she didn't need to be. I was led to her bedroom. Slowly she stripped off my clothes first, pausing to caress my chest, clawing into the hair, whispering, "This is great. Fabulous." And when I was naked, she breathed, "Your turn."

I obligingly removed the blue knit shirt and bra. A bra-burner Sally might have been in principal but she always wore one to disguise the peculiar configuration of her breasts. When bare, each of the nipples angled outward so that, when the nipples were erect, it appeared that each was a small thumb pointing at her left and right biceps. As I slipped off her blue shorts and then underpants, I noted that the pale brown pubic hair remained thin and I idly wondered if it had been worn off from constant use of the orifice.

Three times that evening, interrupted only briefly by oysters Rockefeller, and twice the next—those trysts in the basement recreation room in deference to the senior Beckers' presence—I pounded into Sally who was her usual super-orgasmic self. But something increasingly disturbed me. Gradually I identified and focused on the source of my mental discomfiture amongst pleasure. With each entanglement, I was seeing more clearly Fishbein in those clutches, realizing that I was no longer visualizing Sally Becker. In other words, as I made my final thrusts of Saturday night, I understood that I was not just taken by my collaborator in Astoria, she possessed me. I walked home feeling vaguely uncomfortable and, yes, frightened.

Mother heard, apparently had been listening for, my key in the door lock and opened the door beaming. "Did you have a good time?"

"Just great," I assented, wondering what would happen to her opinion of the decent girl if I told her that yes, I had a very good time tonight fucking Sally twice, but I had had a better time the night before because we fornicated three times. I had no intention of saying anything of the sort to my mother, partly because she would be offended, but mainly because she would not believe me, or if she did, it would be assumed I had used wicked male aggression upon the poor girl's essential innocence.

I started up the stairs. Mother said with off-hand distaste, "Oh, Roy. That girl called you."

"Who? Fishbein?"

She nodded and started back toward the kitchen where the tea kettle could be heard whistling.

"Mind if I use the phone in your room?"

"Go ahead," she said harshly, over her shoulder.

* * * *

"About time you called," Fishbein informed me.

"I just got home."

"I called this morning."

"Well, Mother just now told me. Sorry."

"That figures. Protecting her son from fast women."

"So she thinks. What's up?"

"Nothing. Does something have to be up for us to talk? Tell me how you made out with Sally-next-door. Did you two hold hands? Maybe a kiss or two? Get real lucky and get your hand in her bra?"

I was annoyed. "To be brutally honest, my inquisitor, her name is, in fact, Sally but Friday night I screwed her three times and twice tonight. It's even possible that, as we speak, her fluids may not yet have dried on my genitals."

A silence. Then: "Damn you, Chandler! Damn you!" A quavering voice in the second "Damn you" suggested emotion other than anger.

"You asked."

"Am I supposed to believe you?"

"That's up to you. But I will also volunteer the information that it was this particular Sally who greedily stole away my virginity some years ago."

"The bitch! And your mother approves of her?"

"Only because she's never actually caught us in the act and Sally comports herself to the world as the soul of propriety."

"A preppy, huh? Is she prettier than me?" Her voice was low, smoky.

"No, my dear Fishbein, she isn't."

"Should I still look to see you tomorrow?"

"Sure. What time?"

"Whenever you get here. Bye."

Sunday dinner was predictable fricasseed chicken and served at the traditional hour of five o'clock. Nevertheless, I was wolfishly hungry, this being the result of my mother's subtle punishment for my refusal to accompany her to church following which she always went to a restaurant for brunch. Since finger foods were few in Helen Chandler's larder, I had eaten only a bowl of Cheerios and milk and that at eight in the morning.

"Goodness, Roy, you must be starving!" Mother admonished smugly.

"I didn't have an opportunity to scarf up eggs Benedict off a fat buffet in a fancy restaurant like you did."

"Well, I asked you to come along."

"Sure, so I could feel like a derelict at a Salvation Army mission, having to sing stupid hymns before the food is served. No, thank you. I realize and appreciate your concern for my immortal soul, but before I dress up in a suit to listen to a sanctimonious fool's sermon, I'll just fast. That's a holy thing to do."

Mother looked unhappily guilty.

"Now, if you will excuse me," I threw my wadded linen napkin onto the dining room table, "I have an engagement tonight."

"Are you going over to Sally's?"

"No, I'm going over to Gladys Fishbein's."

"I see. Will you be out late?"

"It isn't likely. I have to go to work tomorrow."

I supposed, I thought as I drove south on Bruckner Boulevard—soon to be Expressway—and across the Whitestone Bridge, I had been somewhat harsh and abrupt with my mother. Invariably she provoked my outbursts and the predictable post-tirade guilt. But it was my life to live or to screw up, not hers.

14

As I climbed the sweltering August Astoria stairway, I felt giddy and free. There was no reason why I should have felt this way. All through Queens the Plymouth had begun to stall each time I let my foot off the accelerator, vastly complicating driving and once almost getting me rear-ended by a delivery truck manned by an angry black man.

Reaching the third floor, I heard the clatter of the typewriter beyond Fishbein's door. Once admitted, I exclaimed, "Christ! How can you stand being cooped like this?" I cranked open the windows. Two Camels competed in burning themselves to nothingness in the ashtray. The floor was littered with wadded paper. Fishbein herself barely acknowledged my arrival. Just a brief smile and a vague wave of her arm, suggesting that the cubicle was mine, to help myself. The refrigerator was bare save for ten or so bottles of beer. I took one, opened it, had a swig and returned to her side. "When," I demanded, "did you last eat something?"

She shrugged. "Last night? No, I guess it was Saturday afternoon. Two slices of pizza. It wasn't worth a shit." The voice was abstracted. I could have been the plumber.

"Are you going to talk to me? This kind of casual interest I could have gotten back at City Island."

She typed a few more words, then stopped to tap a Camel

before lighting it and turning away from her typewriter to give me her attention. "You look tired," she observed.

"I am. After all, spending the weekend wildly screwing your childhood sweetheart is exhausting and I'm not as much in practice as I might be."

She put her cigarette down in the ashtray and rose. "You son of a bitch, Chandler." Her voice was not loud, but with venomous intensity that might as well have been a scream.

"I thought you would appreciate forthrightness."

She took a menacing step forward. I instinctively pressed my knees together. Although she was barefoot, I sensed she could deliver a masterful wallop to my groin. Since she did not speak, just stood in the center of the room glaring at me, I studied her. She had her hands on her hips; her thick hair was in a pony tail, her stance accentuated the full breasts clearly loose beneath the thin white blouse and her very brief blue shorts. Fishbein's options were attack or ridicule or rebuke, but she did none of those. Instead, she dropped to her knees before me and, her elbows on my thighs, held out her hands to me imploringly, eyes serious and sad. She said:

"Please lie to me from now on. If you're not interested in me, just say so. I've spent all week missing you and all you can do is brag about your sexual prowess. Well, congratulations." She tossed her hair and methodically unbuttoned her top. The bare breasts were beyond magnificent; just as I'd conceptualized, they were high and full, nipples large even in repose and areolas wide brown discs. "Could she offer this?" It was spoken quietly; a matter-of-fact question.

"No, Fishbein. Never. But you're not offering, you're displaying."

"There's a difference?"

"A big one. Could be the biggest in the world."

She nodded, looked away, then said: "Will you kiss me now?

The way you did a week ago?"

I have never thought myself to be an unreasonable person, so I leaned forward placing my palms tentatively on the lower swell of the bases of each breast. Before I could kiss her, she whispered with tender roughness, "Go on, Chandler, I want you should touch them." Then our lips met and my hands glided upward. By the time my grasp was on her nipples they were stiff and bulging. One might suppose that I ought to have been too preoccupied to mull over the character and personality of the woman I was kissing and fondling, but such was not the case. In an instant I focused upon her with anatomical clarity. This was an educated, cultivated, deep feeling woman who could not, would not, drive away the vestiges of a Brooklyn heritage. She was grasping yet yielding. Confident but terrified. A human, earthy paradox. And I was in love with her.

The kiss ended. "That was a superb interlude, Chandler, but we have work to do. Now look. The way we ought to pursue this is obvious. I do research and you write it up." She said this as she carefully rebuttoned her top. "This has potential. Trust me. Go through this card file. You'll see that I know what I'm doing." She went to the desk and picking up a small gray metal box handed it to me. Inside were index cards containing neatly typed biographical information.

"Where did you get all this?"

"I spent two long days at the main public library downtown. Believe me, those stone lions by the steps know me so well, they grin when they see me coming."

"It's good, Fishbein, but it isn't enough. I need more depth, so I can get a feel for the subjects as real humans. So each one will be different to the reader. Otherwise all we'll end up with is a dry collection of biographical sketches. People can get that information from the library."

"So you could do better? How are we going to get information so you can, as you put it, make them human? We can't afford to travel all over the fucking country. Besides, half the women we are talking about are dead."

"That's another thing," I said, "Who are we talking about? We need to brainstorm, before going off half-cocked. Who do we want to include and why? Most people our age think Doris Day is an old-time *performer.* We need to set limits. List who we want to profile first. In other words, Fishbein the poet, we need to get organized. I'm not saying we have to be locked into anything, or that we can't bend our rules, but we—or at least I—need a starting point, ground rules."

"Yeah? I guess you want to be the one to decide who gets included, right?" She was leaning negligently against the window casing, an amused look on her face. Then she went to the kitchen.

I called after her, "I *said* brainstorm. That takes two people."

"That means argue," she hurled back. Then she sat down next to me and handed me one of the two bottles of beer she was holding.

"It doesn't have to. Look, I've got an idea. Once we've decided the general types we want to do, each of us will make a list of names. Any that show up on both lists, we definitely include. Others, just on one, we'll talk about."

"Fair enough. All right, now they have to be singers, agreed?"

I nodded. "But not necessarily actresses. And I would say those who were stars or had their greatest fame between 1925 and 1940."

"There may have to be some exceptions there, Chandler."

"I know. I've already said we're not locked into anything." Draining my beer, I glanced at my watch, surprised to see that it was nearly ten o'clock. Then I remembered the car. "Oh shit! I forgot to tell you the car has something wrong with it."

"Jesus! Everything mechanical you touch turns to shit, Chandler. What's the matter with it?"

"Every time I take my foot off the gas pedal it stalls."

She waved her hand dismissively. "Just garbage in the carburetor. If it wasn't dark, I'd fix it tonight. I'll do it in the morning."

"That isn't helping me get home."

She looked astonished. "You were leaving tonight?"

"I'd planned to."

Fishbein turned away. "Oh." Then she abruptly whirled on the sofa to face me. "So you didn't understand?"

"Understand?"

She put her hands gently on my shoulders, "About when I told you to kiss me, told you to touch me. That I wanted we should be lovers."

"Lovers," I repeated, thinking irrelevantly that the term was rather quaint, even archaic.

"I promise it won't be like before. There are hundreds of things you could teach me and things I've thought up I can show you. Go on. Go call, Chandler."

Mother didn't sound annoyed or unhappy, just as though she knew my call would be coming. All she said after a brief resigned sigh was, "All right, Roy. Thank you for letting me know."

Returning to the living room, I lit a cigarette and gazed through the window at a street scene that was typically Queens. A few people walked along the sidewalk, no doubt denizens of the many shabby apartment buildings. At the nearest corner neon lights flaunted the tempting wares of a pizza parlor. In the distance, a traffic light kept up its monotonous changing for the benefit of virtually no motor vehicles. Somewhere, in an apartment on another floor, a baby was crying. Then, "Come on, Chandler. Turn off the light and come here. Stop playing hard to get."

"Just a second." I mashed out my cigarette, switched off the table lamp then fumbled my way to the bedroom. The only lights were a yellow glow from a night light in the bathroom and blue-white streetlight rays shining in through chinks in the venetian blinds. I checked my pocket for the last survivor from my weekend's excesses. But as my eyes adjusted to the dimness, I saw her lying on her back, a pillow elevating her head as she smoked and seemed to be studying me. Even in the near darkness, it was the most arousing body I had ever seen.

"You ought to at least have your shirt off by now," she said testily.

It took me all of ten seconds to strip off everything. I got into bed and leaned over and kissed her murmuring, "Is that better?"

"No, it isn't!" she barked violently, extinguishing her cigarette, sparks flying. "It's all wrong! It's like I'm seducing you. It should be the other way around! I don't care about morality or sinfulness! Fuck morals! Fuck sin!" She jounced off the bed and stood at the window with her back to me, surely not looking out at Astoria; the blinds were too tightly drawn.

And in that instant, I knew what was wrong and what I had to do to rectify it and I felt no revulsion. I stood behind her placing my hands on her shoulders and began to kiss each inch of her scarred back. Although uneven, the surfaces were soft and warm. With my caresses I was absolving the hurt and the shame and the ugliness, not just for me, but for her—however temporarily—as well. At the same time I guided my hands onto her breasts gently squeezing and kneading them, the nipples growing taut and, from the wetness, I realized she was silently weeping. As I continued kissing downward to her narrow waist, I rubbed the muscular stomach, felt the indentation of her naval and, as I began to kiss the cheeks of her buttocks, I rubbed the soft skin of her inner thighs with one hand and, with the other, the thick hair of her heavily bulging pubis, running gently into her vaginal groove, it too wet, but not from tears. Her legs began to tremble and she stumbled to the bed and groped between my legs and grasped me and breathed, "Go on, Chandler. Put it on, darling. Do it."

There was some resistance to my initial thrust. I hesitated, but she whispered, "Push. Hard as you can." I heard an indrawn gasp of pain and then I was in her, pumping rhythmically. To avoid climaxing I thought of mundane things such as the grimy, torn headliner of the Plymouth and Mrs. Horowitz at Sammy Shinbaum's and even my mother peering censoriously around the corner into the bedroom. But after I sensed she had come twice and was about to have a third orgasm, I lost control. Our tongues darted into each others mouths, I held her swaying breasts and sucked the hard tips as she kissed me wildly anywhere she could make contact. Our synchronized releases came, her strong legs gripping me tightly.

"That's the way I've dreamed it would be Chandler; my darling." She continued kissing me even when I'd withdrawn.

After we had each smoked a cigarette in post-coital silence, she asked, "Will you...can you...do it again?"

"I could but that was my last rubber. There's always tomorrow night."

"I don't want to wait. I want to get up on my hands and knees. Have it from behind. Hard. I'll spray in more foam. Please?"

"No, Fishbein," I said firmly, quietly, "I don't want any guilt trip laid on me."

We slept together nude. Toward morning, she began massaging my genitals, but I turned over and she slapped my butt and muttered, "Fuck you, Chandler," and I guessed she went back to sleep; I did.

* * * *

The sassy Fishbein of the morning was a vastly transformed being. She yelled, "Get your lazy, fucking ass up, Chandler! Coffee and bagels are here and you need to get ready for work!"

"Coming, slave-driver. Can I use your shower?"

"Help yourself. If you want to shave, the blade is new. Watch out."

Nursing a trickle of blood, I came to the tacky dinette table. A mug of coffee was placed before me; the bagels were in a bag on the table. She said, "The milk was spoiled, sorry. I fixed the car. Junk in the carburetor like I said. But I even pulled the gas line and blew it out. Any more trouble it has to be sediment in the tank. No problem. I'll pull it and have it flushed out."

"You amaze me, Fishbein."

"No big deal. Mechanical things were meant to serve us, not control us. I intend to maintain the relationship." She paused.

"I'm counting on you to get the things for tonight."

"How many?"

"Oh, God! Two? Five? Ten? Whatever you can handle." When I didn't answer, she grinned briefly and said nervously, "You decide."

I smoked a Marlboro and sipped hot coffee.

She asked suddenly, with staccato quickness. "When are you going to get your stuff?"

"Stuff? What the hell are you talking about?"

"Clothes, razor, after-shave. Stuff."

"Why?"

"Look, Chandler," she threw out her hand intending logic. "There is no sense in your working days two miles away in the Bronx, then driving home to City Island every day, and coming back in the evenings. Think about it. We're collaborators, we're on a project. Be sensible. Just stay here."

It did make sense, especially after the night just past, but how could I explain the rationality to Mother? Suddenly I didn't care. I would arrange with Sammy for some time off early in the day. If possible, I would pack and just leave a note for Mother. That would be easy and painless, at least for me.

16

I resolved to take on City Island before going to work. It was just eight o'clock on an August morning that boded a humid, super-heated, smoggy New York day. I wasn't due at Sammy's until ten. I ought to be able to get to Mother's—assuming Fishbein really had repaired the car—and back in time for official duty, leaving my things in the car's trunk for the day. If I was delayed, I could call from Mother's house.

The only potential delay I dreaded was an eyeball to eyeball confrontation with Mother. Up until last night, I could say with righteous piety that Fishbein was simply my collaborator and I slept on the sofa. I could not convincingly lie to my mother, nor could I tell her with cavalier candor that I was officially shacking up for the foreseeable future. Of course, whatever I told her or wrote in a letter, she would see through the veneer to the truth and both accept it and loathe it. She was a morally unbending woman.

But I had made my decision. Or had it been made for me? No matter, it was there. It was a simple fact that I was going to begin cohabiting with Gladys Fishbein effective August seventh in the year of our Lord 1975. To my relief, the garage was absent of the noble Pontiac. I packed hurriedly, furtively. To my surprise, save for the suits and sports jackets I was leaving behind, everything I possessed fit comfortably into a medium suitcase and a garment bag. These and my typewriter I carried downstairs after pausing to note that the room, which I was now vacating after nearly fourteen years of occupancy, appeared to be unchanged. The absence of my belongings in no way denuded it. Perhaps it had never been mine; just a spare room in Helen Chandler's house.

Writing the note to Mother proved to be every bit as difficult as I had anticipated. All the wordings I considered seemed banal and asinine and empty. A few were just plain stupid and one, in which I attempted to gloss over the moral implications, read as a foul assignation. I decided on simplicity and wrote essentially that for convenience to work and until the completion of the book, I was going to be sharing my co-author's apartment in Astoria.

That grueling task completed I locked the back door, hit the Cross Bronx Expressway and arrived early for work. Fishbein had wrought wonders on the aging Plymouth. It was running better than ever. Perhaps it was a favorable omen of my new life.

All that day, between customers and laughing at Sammy's ribaldry, I secretly worked on my list. Some were obvious: Mae West, Helen Morgan, Bessie Smith, Jane Froman, Ethel Waters, Ethel Merman. I had no doubt these would be on Fishbein's list as well. Others were more elusive: Ruth Etting, Harriet Hilliard, Kate Smith, Lee Wiley, Alice Faye, Mary Martin, Mildred Bailey, Kay Thompson. The possibilities were nearly boundless.

The things we hadn't decided upon were whether we wanted to include foreign stars and how many we planned to profile in all. We would need to discuss that. Also, next to nothing was known about a few of them. In the instance of Lyda Roberti, for example, even her date of birth was uncertain. We hadn't established as many ground rules as we ought to have. To only feature Americans would exclude such luminaries as Gertrude Lawrence and Marlene Dietrich.

I arrived back at the apartment, stopping only at a drugstore—for an obvious reason—and let myself in using the two keys she had provided me. The temperature I estimated to be ninety-six degrees. I hurriedly opened the windows and turned on a small oscillating fan. Since the Harley hadn't been in the parking lot, I assumed the apartment would be empty, which it was. I took a beer from the otherwise bare refrigerator and sat down two inches from the fan blades. Neither the beer nor the fan provided much relief. I opened my suitcase and extracted a pair of blue terry cloth shorts, deciding I might just as well dress for the tropics.

Also I plucked out a T-shirt which had a faded scene from the Mediterranean and was emblazoned with once red but now pink script announcing "Monaco." Certainly, I had never been to Monaco, nor had either of my parents. The reason I owned the shirt was due to visiting the United Nations on a field trip when I was a senior in high school. It was featured in the gift shop and Monaco seemed to be the most exotic place in the world. And, no, I still haven't gone there.

The unmistakable roar of Fishbein's motorcycle drifted up from the payment and through the open windows. Presently there was a muffled quick thump of feet on stairs; then she burst into the room. That was, to be accurate, unlatching two automatic locks, the extent into which her apartment could be burst. She slapped down the two paper grocery bags on the end table by the sofa, and threw herself on me. I had made the error of standing up when she entered, only to be knocked down onto the couch, her arms around my neck. Incessant, stifling kisses followed. Finally she stopped her attack and cried, "Oh, Chandler! You adorable, beautiful shit! You're here! You came back!" She sat up suddenly. "What did your mother say?"

"No idea. I went over, packed my shit and left a note." I shrugged. "Probably the new will excludes me."

"Do you wish you hadn't done it?"

"I'm here, aren't I?"

"You can change your mind," she said in a very un-Fishbein small voice.

"I could, but I won't. Listen. Let's get down to some basic economics. What should I buy?"

She looked uncertain. "I don't give a shit. The rent is four hundred a month and the utilities are included. I'd have to pay that anyway. You want to, you could buy food, beer." A pause as she stroked my thigh, watching enthralled at the obvious result through my flimsy shorts. "And rubbers. Dozens, hundreds of them. You did get some today, didn't you?"

I snapped my fingers and said in feigned negligence, "Forgot all about them. I'll have to ride you bareback tonight. Trust your foam stuff."

"Like hell you will!" She snatched her evil-looking knife from her boot. "You want to lose it, motherfucker?"

I smiled and tapped the white druggist's bag next to me. "Just kidding. Bought a box of twenty-four. They're cheaper that way."

"There are a few subjects where my sense of humor is wanting," she told me flatly, sliding her knife back into its resting place. She looked down at the bags she had brought in as though noticing them for the first time and, reaching into one, drew out a large canned chow mein dinner with a can of fried noodles taped to the one where sauce and vegetables and probably two or three soggy pieces of chicken swam within. "You want we should eat Chinese tonight?"

"Suits me. How much do I owe you? Groceries are supposed to be my contribution."

"You owe me at least two hard-ons tonight. Food's on me this time."

"Fair enough. You ready to trade lists?"

"Give me a minute to put away this crap and get a beer."

I noticed Fishbein's list was neatly typed and she had even written song titles next to some of the names. Many were the same as I had listed. "Who is Alberta Hunter?" I inquired.

"You've never heard of her? She was a black woman. Very popular in the colored club circuit. But her voice was beautiful, almost operatic, which was not a talent white America wanted then. So she moved to Paris; spent most of her career there. You've never heard of 'My Particular Man'? You know, 'He ain't no boxer, but he can poke. He ain't no swimmer, but he can stroke.' Never heard that?"

I laughed and shook my head. "Never."

She got up and walked over to the stereo, where she opened the record cabinet. "You want to hear it?"

"Sure. Say! Let me look at that record jacket." She handed it to me, and as I read the information which was about several featured artists, she put on the record and adjusted the controls. "Do you have a lot of these?"

Opening the cabinet wide she gestured inside where there must have been over a hundred record albums neatly stacked. Then the music began and I was introduced to the high, delicate, slightly dreamy voice of Alberta Hunter. When the song was over, I asked her to play it again.

"You know, Fishbein, there's a hell of a lot of biographical information on this record jacket. Probably on a lot of them. And if I can hear the singers, I can write with what black people call soul."

"Yeah, but be careful. A lot of these records have been unavailable for years. They're irreplaceable."

"You're telling me you think I'm an ox?"

"I'm telling you to be careful," she qualified tolerantly. She kissed me briefly before sitting back down. "And no, Chandler, I don't think you're an ox." She added salaciously, "Maybe a bull."

"Flattery will get you everywhere."

"Hmm." She was studying my list again. "Who is Harriett Hilliard?"

"She was a singer in Ozzie Nelson's orchestra. You probably know her as Harriett Nelson from the old TV show. Whether they were married when she started performing with his band or at some later time, I just don't know. But the name recognition will be valuable."

"Yeah, sure. After she wasn't singing any more."

"OK, scratch her."

Thus our list was built and culled. Then, jointly, the writing and research and editing process took shape. A few subjects, originally intended to be featured, were axed because too much had already been written about them. Finally we had our list and we worked in usually ambient quiet. Included were: Ruth Etting, Jane Froman and Mildred Bailey; a total of twenty-five artists. Fishbein remarked with satisfaction, "That's a good, workable number. At roughly four thousand words each, that's a hundred thousand word manuscript. Publishers shy away from anything longer. Too expensive to print."

We settled quickly into a daily routine of my job at Sammy's, evenings of writing and typing and amiable intellectual arguments. The canned or frozen food which I bought and Fishbein prepared was adequate.

Our nights were consumed by frantic and imaginative and zestful sexual congress with Fishbein's exquisite foam-filled body joining my anxious latex ensheathed penis. Two encounters were routine; once we had four and that next morning I barely had energy to turn the ignition key of the Plymouth.

The pattern was smashed more quickly than it had been established. On Thursday evening, the telephone bell sounded. Fishbein muttered, "Fuck you," then irritably went to the kitchen. I heard her say, "Sure, he's here; hold the phone."

Oh shit! Mother calling to lay a guilt trip on me, I thought, hurrying to the kitchen. Would she be pleading or the voice of cold morality. I took the receiver from Fishbein's outstretched hand. Her expression was noncommittal. "Hello," I said tentatively.

"Well, well, Roy! How are you, son?"

"Pop! Just fine. Staying busy. How did you get the number here?"

"From your mother," he said evenly, with a tinge of guilt in his voice. So my parents thought the plight of their son to be sufficiently perilous to break their mutual resolve never to communicate with one another. I knew for a fact that in Mother's address book his name was not allowed to contaminate the "C" division, but in the back, in a section called "Notes," was written, "Mr. Arthur Chandler," and Pop's telephone number.

"Oh. Is anything wrong?"

"No. I hope not." He gave a nervous laugh. "I just wondered what you had decided about Sag Harbor. Manny and Sylvia would like to see you and, of course, I would, too."

Hmm, I thought, divide and conquer, but I said, "I don't think I can make it. We're three chapters into our book and..."

"Book? You're writing a book?"

"We are. My friend and I. That's why I'd hate to leave and have her stuck with all the work."

Recklessly he offered, "Bring her along. You two can have the upstairs. Manny and Sylvia can use one of the downstairs bedrooms and I'll take the other. No problem."

"I'm not sure," I told him uncertainly. "I'll ask her. Can I call you back?"

"Absolutely. I'll be here all evening."

Thoughtfully, I put the telephone receiver on its cradle. So if he, in complicity with Mother, couldn't divide he would investigate the nature of the adversary and try to find chinks of vulnerability in her facade. My parents had a viable opponent in Gladys

Fishbein.

"Chandler! Who was that? Your old man?"

"No, it was Martin Luther calling from the grave to request that I accompany Mother to church on Sunday."

"Fuck you!"

"I intend for you to; but let's get a little more work done first."

"Was that your old man?" A hint of exasperation.

"It was."

"What did he want?"

"Have you ever been to the beach before?" I settled next to her on the sofa where she was sorting cards in the file box.

She stopped and said quietly, "Yeah. Once. It's one of my earliest recollections. I must have been five or six years old. My father took us to Rockaway Beach one Saturday. I remember he had on red bathing trunks that ballooned out and I laughed so hard he got embarrassed. Of course, my old lady made me wear shorts and a sleeveless shirt; lied and said she couldn't find a suit my size. We had fun."

"How would you like to go out to Sag Harbor with me this weekend? An all-expenses-paid vacation. We could just relax. Go to the beach. Pop has rented the same cottage for the second and third weeks in August since I was little. You'd like my father."

"No, thanks." She shook her head. "I can't swim."

"You don't have to. Just lie around sun-bathing; looking voluptuous."

"Sure. Think about it, Chandler. Me in a bikini, with my back. Forget it."

"So, wear a T-shirt. Say you burn easily."

"With my Semitic, dark skin? Who'd believe that? No thanks. You go, I don't care."

"Would it mean anything if I told you that I'd like to show you off?"

"Show me off, huh?" She smiled wearily and lit a Camel. "OK, Chandler, darling. Take me and show me off. But, I warn you, some people won't like the fucking show."

"Tough shit. You want to go to Mineola and hitch a ride with Pop?"

"No. We'll take my bike. I want to be able to cut out in a hurry if I don't like what I see coming down."

"Why not the car?"

"You've become too damned confident about that car. Sag Harbor is a long way out on the island if my geography serves. Definitely the bike."

"All right," I agreed unhappily, "the bike."

Fishbein reached over and held my chin gently and kissed me. "Show me off." She spoke dreamily.

"How did you get that little scar below your eye?" I asked suddenly.

A short laugh. "That's the only scar that's my own damned fault. A year or two after we moved to Bayshore—I guess I was ten—there was a cute little boy who used to come to a park next to our apartment building. He was a year or so younger than me, I guess. Anyway, I used to corner him in the baseball backstop and wouldn't let him go until he kissed me. Sometimes he'd cry, but once he was too fast for me and I tripped and caught my cheek on the sharp edge of the chainlink fence. Bled like hell. I never bothered him again. Kid stuff."

With an eerie feeling, recalling Charlotte my nemesis, I called Pop back, telling him we would see them all on Saturday morning.

"Of course you're going to take some condoms with you this weekend, darling." We were sitting propped up in bed drinking our first cup of coffee. Fishbein was always sweetly reasonable during post-coital bliss such as that Saturday morning. She leaned up and kissed my neck, while twining her fingers in mine.

"But why? Surely we can go two days without screwing. Besides after seventy or eighty miles on the back of your motorcycle, I expect to be rendered permanently impotent. Or, at best, too sore to perform."

"I love you, Chandler." It was the first time she had actually verbalized her feelings. I wondered then if she could, in fact, be timorous of the approaching meeting, the confrontation.

"I love you, too," I answered, not exactly rhetorically, because at that particular moment I did, in fact, love her. And I wondered what sort of inquisition Pop and Uncle Manny and Aunt Sylvia and—in absentia—Mother had planned.

She smiled up at me. "Relax. The Long Island Expressway will, I predict, be the smoothest part of this weekend."

"You're a shrewd woman."

*****

Fishbein was right about the Expressway part or else I was developing a knack for being a motorcycle passenger. I could not see the speedometer but, since we passed all other vehicles, I assumed we were speeding. When we stopped for gas near Ronkonkoma I asked, "Aren't you afraid you'll get a ticket?"

"Hah! Only if the bastards catch me, which is not very likely."

"How come? Long Island is a dead-end, so to speak."

"See, I spot one after me, I run it up to about ninety. Cruise the left shoulder, pull off at the first exit, hide in a driveway. It's simple. Motorcycles are hard to catch unless the pig has one, too."

"All right. Change the scenario. Aren't you afraid of getting yourself—let alone me—killed?"

"Nah. You've seen me ride. Have I ever...Hey! You're running the fucking tank over, Acne Albert!" She was addressing the pimply-faced punk attendant, not me.

He put the cap on the tank and said "Ten-fifty," in a surly voice.

"Don't shit me, kid. It's ten forty-eight. *You* ought to see that since you were watching the pump instead of the tank like you should have been doing."

"Don't have no change 'cept quarters."

"Fine. Make it ten twenty-five then. Or walk your ass to the office and get my fifty-two cents." She handed him eleven dollars. He made a bristling retreat.

"Your wining personality at work again, Fishbein."

"I was being nice."

The boy returned and handed her fifty-two pennies, which she in turn hurled in his face. "You little shit! Take my advice: stop jerking off twice a day and maybe your face won't look like the craters of the moon!"

With that we squealed away. I felt a jolt which meant, I realized when I glanced behind me, that Fishbein had run over the kid's foot. Maniacal laughter floated back to me.

As I firmly grasped the narrowest part of the flesh hourglass which was Gladys Fishbein; the place where the sand sifts so slowly, I speculated about human relations during the ensuing holiday. Pop knew what to expect more or less, had even spoken with her briefly on the telephone.

My aunt and uncle were totally unprepared, except by what impressions Mother would no doubt have provided them. Uncle Manny was good natured, unflappable, and admired a voluptuous woman. But Aunt Sylvia was another matter. She was a pretty woman with bleached blond hair who wore too much make-up and could assume airs of snobbery to which she was without legitimate claim. I knew for a fact that when Uncle Manny met her she was working as a waitress in a diner on the Boston Post Road in Mamaroneck, and in that capacity was the only success story in her family.

The longevity of their marriage was due to the craftiness of Uncle Manny in allowing her to think she was the boss by letting her make decisions of little or no importance, while he took all the matters of substance upon himself. For instance, she always insisted that their new Cadillacs be black, because it was "elegant" and "fitting" for a luxury car, which was utter insanity for year-round South Florida residents. Uncle Manny just ordered them black and tempered the finish with white leather interiors and dual air-conditioning.

Incidentally, some years later, Aunt Sylvia amended her position on black cars due to an unfortunate experience one July during a two-hour traffic jam on Federal Highway near Fort Lauderdale when a short in the electrical system caused the air-conditioning and window lifts to malfunction. Thus, it was necessary for them to creep along with the doors open to avoid total suffocation.

*****

Fishbein parked the Harley in the yard. The short driveway

next to the pastel pink cottage contained Pop's Lincoln and Uncle Manny's black Cadillac Fleetwood. After removing her helmet and shaking out her hair, she put her hands on her hips and surveyed the scene critically, saying finally, "Jesus! What is this? Vacation or a mafia funeral?"

So I was not without reservations when I cautiously opened the screen door to the bungalow. The airy room which served as both living and dining space was furnished with colorfully patterned, chintz-upholstered wicker which was approximately the quality imported by the company Otto Becker worked for.

Uncle Manny was sprawled in an armchair asleep with his mouth open which made him look even more stupid than he wasn't. Pop and Aunt Sylvia were seated drinking coffee and looked up with attempts at startled expressions on their faces, which was ridiculous. The Harley must have been audible all the way from Huntington, especially with the windows open. Pop rose quickly and approached us smiling. Aunt Sylvia remained seated, smoking, a look of mocking appraisal on her face.

"Hi, Pop! Aunt Sylvia!" I went over and kissed her cheek, which was returned as well as a pat on my shoulder. "Be nice," I warned in a murmur.

"This is Fishbein, everyone. She got us here from Astoria in an hour. I didn't think it could be done."

"To tell the truth," she said modestly, "It was nearly an hour and half, but I had to stop for gas and," gesturing loosely at me, "I had extra weight. An hour is a possibility." She shook my father's outstretched hand and nodded briefly at my aunt.

Uncle Manny roused and said, "Could it be the goddess of Brooklyn?"

"You got a problem with Brooklyn, Goofy?" She took off her leather jacket revealing clear hints of her stunning body, not lost on my uncle. Sylvia glared at Fishbein and Pop looked helplessly at me.

"It's Manny, my dear. Uncle Manny," I said quickly.

"I know. But I want to call him Uncle Goofy. It's cute. So I'm a Brooklyn girl already. You have something against that?"

He was looking at her tits, but said, laughing, "No, young lady, I don't have any problem with either Brooklyn or Uncle Goofy!"

Everyone laughed except Sylvia who lit another cigarette she'd fitted into her holder. She asked, "Would you like a cup of coffee, Roy?"

"Both of us would," Fishbein told her, lighting a Camel from a stick match lit by striking it against the tread of one of her boots. She sniffed. "Something smells good."

Pop said, "That's my celebrated New England clam chowder cooking. Fresh clams, fresh milk, butter, even fresh Long Island potatoes."

"You did take the clams out of the shells?" Fishbein asked conversationally, favoring him with one of her glittering smiles.

"I think I got them all, but be careful the first few times you bite down. I'm getting old and careless."

She studied him and then proclaimed frankly, "I'd guess that twenty or thirty years ago, you were as good looking as your son."

"Better looking," he assured her and gave a real grin.

Seated at the table, coffee before us, Aunt Sylvia spoke for the first time. "What do you do, Miss Fishbein?"

"I'm a writer."

"She writes poetry," I put in.

"How interesting. Have you written anything that I might have read?"

"I doubt it. You don't impress me as anyone who would like poetry."

She glared at Fishbein, then at me, and said to Pop, "Just like Helen said," and left the table to go sit by Uncle Manny.

"I'm assuming that Helen is the former Mrs. Chandler," she deduced, addressing my father. "So what exactly did she say? Let me guess. How about an uncouth and trashy Brooklyn Jew-girl who is a serious threat to the morals and propriety of her precious son?"

"Cool it, Fishbein," I said quickly.

"No, Roy. It's all right. Yes, to be honest, that is roughly what Helen said, but it doesn't mean I'm saying it." He laughed shortly. "Maybe that's the reason we didn't stay married."

Fishbein leaned over and hugged Pop briefly. "Now I know where Chandler gets it from, why I love him."

"Aunt Sylvia?" I called. "Be honest. Have you ever read any poetry?"

"Ah…well, no."

"Good. I think poetry stinks myself. So what's the gripe?"

She smiled. "None, I guess. I know someone who does read it, though. Uncle Goofy, here." She patted his arm, then returned to the table. "Why don't we all walk down to the bay? Do you want to put on a bathing suit? The water is marvelous. I was in first thing this morning.

"I didn't bring a bathing suit, but I wouldn't mind the walk," Fishbein said.

"She can't swim," I said quickly. "I think she's afraid of the water."

"I'm not afraid of a fucking thing, Chandler." Apparently my help was unwelcome.

Pop burst out laughing and left the room saying, "I've got to stir the chowder before we go."

We strolled past rows of garishly decorated cottages toward the bay. Pop and Sylvia and I walked several paces behind Uncle Manny-Goofy who had engaged Fishbein in a rather involved discussion about cadences and pentameters which she seemed to enjoy.

"Are you in love with her?" Aunt Sylvia asked with her usual candor.

"She says she's in love with me," I replied evasively. "We work well together."

"Yes, and she's a very handsome young woman, but you did not answer my question."

"I'm just not sure."

Pop had been walking along in silent discomfiture, but with a touch of bitterness, he then said: "Well, just make sure you are." Then more mildly, "Your mother didn't like her especially."

I laughed, more a snort. "Fishbein didn't put it as mildly. And Mother must have thought I was in grave danger for her to have called you."

"We don't talk often," he admitted.

"But what is bothering her most is our living arrangements, right?"

"She did mention that." Pop was uncomfortable.

Aunt Sylvia seemed not to be listening, so I said, "Maybe that's what you and Mother ought to have done. Would have saved you a lot of misery."

"Might have, but I'm glad we didn't."

"Why not?"

"Because, well, I don't want to sound maudlin, but then we wouldn't—I wouldn't—have you." He smiled briefly.

Quickening her pace, Sylvia caught up with Manny and circled his arm with hers. "I don't want you to be stolen away by this young temptress. We just celebrated our silver anniversary last month."

"Gee, honey, we were talking poetry. That's safe enough, isn't it?"

"Aren't most poems about love?"

"Not mine," Fishbein informed her and dropped back to a position between Pop and me. She leaned over and kissed Pop's cheek. "Thanks for including me, whatever the motivation. I needed a change of scenery. This is a quaint place. You two Chandlers know something?"

My father smiled and replied jocularly, "Between the two of us, I'd say that we possess one or two pearls of wisdom."

"This is the first time I've ever been out of New York City. In my life."

"I've known a lot of people like that," Pop said. "It's a cult city. I have a fraternity brother who hasn't left Manhattan in almost twenty-five years. We have lunch together once or twice a year. I've heard that New Orleans and San Francisco are that way, too. It's funny. You think of small town people as being provincial, but it happens in big cities, too."

Now we were approaching the harbor and the beach. Hundreds of sailboats were flitting about, while an armada of dissimilar motorboats warily tried to avoid them. The sand was accented by a psychedelically colorful mixture of bathing suits and beach umbrellas. A classic Long Island summer Saturday, the sun bright and a pleasant, cooling breeze.

Fishbein asked, "Is that Long Island Sound? I'd have thought it would be bigger."

I shook my head. "This is just Peconic Bay. It leads out to the Sound. See? There aren't any waves."

She nodded, watching Manny and Sylvia strip off beach robes and run into the water. Pop followed their lead, trotting across the sand. I made to follow, but she gripped my forearm urgently. "Please don't! Stay with me."

"No one hinted you should go in. I won't be long. Here's a bench you can sit on."

"No! Don't leave me, Chandler!" Her voice was at once violent and pleading. "You don't understand."

"I guess I don't."

Her eyes were wide, fearful. "You remember my telling you about the time my old man took us to Rockaway Beach? That it was one of my earliest recollections? Do you know why?"

"No."

She subsided against me on the bench, weeping. "My old lady tried to drown me that day." Her voice was a stage whisper. "Please stay with me here."

An urge, a strong one, dictated that I ignore the entreaty; that I just forget she was with me, and dive into the water. But her wistful request left me weak, unable to act or to move. Why had she come at all? And, too, what made me unable to deny her pleadings? Perhaps, as I had told her four hours ago, I was in love with her. But if that were true, why did I have no feeling of elation, just a nagging dread tinged with fear. Conversely, perhaps this was how love really felt and all I had experienced previously was simply infatuation or base lust. I asked, "Have you ever been in love?"

She studied me a moment, looked away and said, "Never. Not until now." Then she lit a cigarette and added, "And it scares the hell out of me."

"Why?"

"I'm afraid I'll screw it all up. That I'll hurt you. And, yeah, that I'll hurt me, too."

I shrugged, "It's always risky. Love is a form of collaboration like our book. Business partners take risks every day."

"You're a true fucking romantic, Chandler. Come on, I've had enough nautical scenery. Let's use that sundeck I spied back at Pop's house. We can get a little work done."

I nodded, but made no comment that "your old man" was now "Pop." I got my father's attention, gestured that we were leaving to which he nodded, waved and jumped back into the slightly ruffled, azure water that was Peconic Bay.

I had always liked the sundeck myself. It could be reached either by an exterior stairway or by a doorway at the end of the sloped-ceiling second floor.

Beneath the deck was a screened porch. The second floor of the cottage had been left open with the exception of a small bathroom. Many of the tenants who rented the house had young children, so this sleeping loft was ideal.

Fishbein and I took our bags from the storage boot of the Harley and went upstairs using the interior staircase. Once upstairs, she studied the chamber and said, "This is nice." Then, frowning, she dropped her duffel bag and went over to the bed. "Just one little problem to rectify," and she began dragging the bed across the floor, kicking the colorful but impeding hooked rugs away.

"What in hell are you doing?"

"Use your head, Chandler. This bed was right over the downstairs bedrooms. You want everyone should be able to *hear* what they assume—correctly—that we'll be doing tonight? I don't want Auntie Sylvia counting *strokes*, for christsake!"

"You're a devious woman, but have you considered the possibility that you may be a nymphomaniac?"

"Not a chance. I'm just making up for lost time. You've got me to age thirteen. There's another ten to be accounted for. Think you're up to it?"

"Yeah, but I may die trying."

"What could be better than to die of screwing?"

"That's a good point; pun was intended."

We settled into deck chairs close to one another and began writing; in the case of Fishbein it was to copy her scrawled notes, transforming them into the neatly printed index cards from which I wrote the chapters for the book. Just then, in the absence of a typewriter, I was writing on a steno pad:

Chapter 5: Glad Rag Doll

In 1896, in the small wheat-farming community of David City, Nebraska, was born the star who would be called at various points in her rather brief career, "the Recording Sweetheart," "the Happy Singer of Sad Songs," "the Sweetheart of Columbia Records" and ultimately, "the Queen of All Torch Singers." These were the accolades rightfully bestowed upon Ruth Etting.

Some sources say she went to Chicago as early as 1913 to study at the Chicago Academy of Arts. For several years, she also worked as a designer and hat maker at a millinery shop belonging to Maybelle Weil whose husband, Milton Weil, was a music publisher. He was impressed by her beauty and talent and was able to influence the owners of the Rainbow Gardens to hire Ruth as a chorus girl. She worked for a number of years in various clubs but rarely as a single artist.

It was not until 1926—according to Miss Etting 1925—before she began singing for recordings, the first of which was "Hello Baby" backed up by the Art Kohn band. Whichever year it was, it launched a career which took her to New York in late 1926.

She was most comfortable when recording with the single piano back-up of Rube Bloom but…

"I'll be damned!" Fishbein murmured, "I didn't know that."

"What?"

"About Ethel Merman."

"What about her? You do all the research."

"Yeah, but I just copy things. It's not until I write the cards that I study the information."

"So? What about Ethel Merman?"

"I always assumed she was a Jew. She isn't. In fact, her father was a Lutheran storekeeper. Her first singing was in the church choir. Later she was the church secretary until her career took off."

"Hmm. I'd have guessed she was Jewish, too."

"Sorry for the interruption."

"No problem." I drifted back to writing.

...but Ruth could sing to larger accompaniments when necessary and was equally excellent.

Unlike many performers profiled in this writing, Miss Etting was never the slave of drink or drugs or stardom itself, but rather fell victim to a mob-related character—one Moe Snyder, known as "the Gimp"—albeit a willing victim. It was he who largely steamrollered her career to its heights, probably higher than she ever wished it to go. For by 1937, at the age of forty-one, she turned her back on all the glitter and "retired" to an isolated ranch near Colorado Springs.

Nevertheless, Ruth Etting made those few years count enormously in the annals of popular music including stage, screen, radio and recordings. She became famous for the repopularization of the old Nora Bayes and Jack Norworth happy tune, "Shine on Harvest Moon."

But songs which she could inure with her innate pathos as her metier such as "Love Me or Leave Me"—later the title of a motion picture loosely based upon her life—and the difficult Rodgers and Hart number "Ten Cents a Dance" were classic Ruth Etting, mirroring her own bizarre and melodramatic personal life.

"Lunch is served!" Pop called up the stairs. Those words took me back to my childhood. It seemed to me that Pop always did the cooking when we were on vacation. He had adopted the practice of calling up the stairs when I was just five or six, respecting my privacy. Just like he always knocked on my bedroom door when we were a family in Mineola. Sadness welled up in me and just for an instant Fishbein, rising and stretching her magnificent body, seemed alien and almost ludicrous on the sundeck in Sag Harbor.

At the table, neatly set for five, a bowl of oyster crackers for a centerpiece, Manny and Sylvia were seated over their bowls of steaming chowder like Pavlovian dogs. Sounds of kitchen activity meant my father had heard us on the stairs and was ladling out our meal. I could picture him sprinkling pepper on the filled bowls and adding a pat of butter for richness.

"What's wrong?" Fishbein asked brightly, "Isn't it fit to eat?"

"We were waiting for you." Sylvia said acidly and added, "Trying to be polite."

"That's nice of you. When you're used to eating alone like I have most of my life, your manners go to the dogs." I was relieved. Another potential confrontation glossed over by Fishbein.

"Roy!" Pop called. "There's beer and iced tea in here. My hands are full. Sylvia's having mineral water."

I gestured to Manny. "How about you? Iced tea or beer? It's beer for us."

"Then I'll have one, too."

Fishbein sat next to Manny and looked into his bowl. As I went into the kitchen, I heard her exclaim, "Damn! That must be a thousand calories!"

Aunt Sylvia remarked cattily, "Don't worry. I'm sure you'll work them off."

"What's the fuck's that supposed to mean?"

"I mean…"

"You meant that you're assuming I'm screwing your nephew and you're one hundred percent correct."

"Uh-oh," I murmured to Pop.

Fishbein was warming to her topic. "In fact, I predict two couplings tonight, but don't worry about your beauty sleep being disturbed, I've already moved the bed so it won't be over your room."

"Soup's on!" Pop declared in a loud voice, rushing into the

melee. The arena. I followed, carrying beer.

"What's your book about?" Uncle Manny asked quickly to change the subject.

I explained the project briefly and began reeling off names.

"Jane Froman!" Aunt Sylvia interrupted, sounding thrilled. "Remember, Manny? We saw her in a concert when we were on our honeymoon."

"You're right, dear. I do remember."

"This stuff is good," Fishbein told my father. "I've never had any before. Regardless of my name, I only rarely eat any kind of fish or seafood. To tell the truth, I don't usually like it."

Aunt Sylvia asked suddenly, "Speaking of names, what is your first name? Surely you have one."

"I do, but I don't answer to it. It happens to be Gladys. If you're uncomfortable calling me 'Fishbein,' try 'Miss' Fishbein. Even 'Hey, you' is all right with me."

"What do your parents do?" Uncle Manny inquired.

"As far as I know, decompose, if they aren't through decomposing already. They're both dead." Since her voice had been grimly remorseless, no one offered any condolences.

Pop asked, "What do you two want to do this afternoon? Are there any sights you'd like to see?"

"I'm definitely going to take a swim," I said, ignoring Fishbein's glare, then I'm going to get back to Ruth Etting. I was sort of on a roll before lunch."

He turned to Fishbein, "How about you? Can I take you on a grand tour?"

"I'd like that," she said, somewhat to my surprise, and gave me a smug grin.

So, as I walked briskly to the beach I had only my own thoughts for company. Well, almost. Part way to the bathing area, the green Lincoln cruised by and Pop gave a short blast of the horn and his passenger gave a cute un-Fishbein wave of her hand. She, the utter embodiment of liberated womanhood, still knew the tricks of the past in pitting son against father, man against man. Not that I seriously suspected my father would pull off the road in some obscure beachfront locale for a sandy tryst with Fishbein. It was just the symbolism.

But I grew up that afternoon. I have often told that to my wife of over twenty years. She doesn't agree or disagree for that was my personal experience and it cannot be shared except in the most vicarious way.

Sag Harbor and the cottage held memories that were precious to me. There, even my parents' disintegrating romance was given a hiatus. It was true even during that last summer when, no doubt, the dissolution papers had already been filed.

I had been wrong in bringing Fishbein here. She was an unsettling distraction to a window into my past. I felt as though I was nude and that I had allowed too much of myself to be revealed. But hadn't Fishbein already shown her essence by saying "Chandler" and then exposing her ruined back? Was I entitled to secrets from her?

Love would come hard to her despite the fact that she declared it so earnestly to me and I had reaffirmed it, verbally, without reservation. As I dove into the rippling waters of Peconic Bay, I wondered if my scars were deeper because they were within rather than being on display, like Fishbein's. And she could choose to show them or not as she saw fit.

In bed that night, the first of the two predicted fornications concluded, Fishbein said, "I thought you said you weren't rich. Your father rents this place and drives a fancy car."

"I didn't say we were poor. We always had food to eat. I don't think you ever went hungry."

"Only the times when my old lady locked me in the closet for the day. Those times I got hungry."

"Oh."

The remainder of the weekend was a droll tragicomedy symbolized by our departure with Aunt Sylvia remaining in the house, Uncle Manny standing in the doorway his arm raised in tentative benediction and Pop in the yard waving in frantic joyousness as the Harley ripped away from the interlude.

Two milestones, really three, caused great celebration in the Astoria apartment the last week of August. The third item was unrelated to aesthetics but was the most remunerative which, by the way, is a truism of virtually all artistic efforts. I received a check, forwarded by my mother, in the amount of six hundred fifty dollars for settlement of the insurance claim on my stolen VW. Then Fishbein received a contract on her poetry collection which she ecstatically waved in my face as I walked in from the day at Sammy's.

"Take a look, Chandler!" She shouted, then kissed me violently.

I studied the contract, which was from a firm called Greenfields Press and which I had never before heard of. They were offering her, as best I could glean from the unfamiliar legal jargon, a five hundred dollar advance against ten percent royalties on gross and that the initial print run would be five thousand copies. "Nice going, Fishbein, but isn't five hundred lean for a whole book of poems?"

She looked annoyed, probably because my enthusiasm failed to match her own. "It's a damn good advance for poetry," she answered sharply. Then her eyes brightened and she gave me her glittering smile. "Here. This came for you."

I took the envelope she handed me and, before opening it,

saw that it was from "Music Memories" in Lisbon, Indiana. The stationery was pale blue and of heavy weight.

"Open the fucking thing!" Fishbein commanded.

I tore it open and studied the message which read, in summary, that they were pleased to inform me that my piece was timely and insightful; that they would like to feature it in their January issue and they were willing to pay five hundred dollars for first serial rights provided I signed and returned the enclosed agreement, in which case they would send a check "forthwith."

Fishbein had been leaning over behind me with her forearms on my shoulders and her chin resting on my head reading the letter. Normally I hate people reading over my shoulder, but I was so elated I would have gladly mounted a loudspeaker on the top of the black Plymouth and driven it all over Astoria rereading the letter to all who would listen.

"Jesus," she whispered hoarsely, "that's fantastic. Not just the money, either."

"I got stuck on the money part."

"The best thing is they only want to buy first serial rights so we can still use the Zuma Alcorn piece as our first chapter."

"Why couldn't we use it anyway?"

"Shit, Chandler! You don't know from nothing." She lit a Camel in quick exasperation. "See. If they had bought *all* rights, you would have to get permission from them to reuse it in the book which might cost you more than they're *paying* you. Either that or you'd have to do a rewrite."

"I'll be damned. You know a lot about this business."

"Believe me, it pays to know. There's another good part to that offer."

"What's that?"

"The outfit is paying on acceptance. Most periodicals, even the super-slick ones, pay on publication. That means you get your money now, not in January." She paused, took a final draw on her cigarette and extinguished it, a thoughtful look on her face. "You do understand, this book we're writing is not best-seller material. If a publisher takes it, the advance will be small and my guess is they will try to make it big and glossy, for the carriage trade. So they put a high cover price on it to compensate for limited anticipated sales. Do you understand what I'm telling you?"

"That I shouldn't quit my job at Sammy's?"

She leaned over and kissed me. "Not just that. Look, with your talent, you ought to shoot for fucking mass market. See? Maybe a novel. Even the Zuma Alcorn book your heart's set on isn't something that will sell big."

"No, but I want to do it."

"But don't you want to be well known?"

"Jesus, Fishbein, this sounds almost like my mother telling me to get a decent job. Are you also going to lecture me about finding a nice girl to settle down with?"

She laughed after an initial angry glare. "No. I like you unsettled down with a not-nice girl."

"Well, I have no plans to start anything until we finish this project. But a novel? Get real, Fishbein. For christsake, what about?"

"Maybe us."

"Us? A three hundred and twelve page orgasm?"

"There's more to us than screwing, I hope."

"Yes, but a lot of things you wouldn't want printed. Would you?"

By answer she snatched the "Musical Memories" envelope from my hand and studied it, frowning. "Someone opened this before. See? Does your old lady open your mail?"

"I didn't think so."

"Let me see that insurance company envelope. You still have it?"

I nodded, dug in the desk drawer designated as "mine" and handed it to her.

"This has been opened, too. So, she is a devious bitch after all."

"How can you tell? I mean that those were opened before."

"Look at the way it's sealed. There's a slight overlap. I can always tell." She shrugged. "If it doesn't piss you off, I don't care, either." Then, "What are you going to do with your new riches?"

"Buy a car," I answered impulsively, without hesitation, then amended, "That is when I get the rest of the money."

"Fuck that. We'll go looking tomorrow. When you get the money, you can pay me back. You sure you don't want a bike? Cheap on gas."

"Not my style. I want a car, one that has nothing worth stealing."

"As I recall, your Volkswagen had nothing worth stealing, but they got it anyhow. Where do you want to go? Obviously, not here in the city. It's all trash."

"How about over in Nyack?" I suggested. "Lots of old people trade in cars as a habit. Not when the city has ruined them, destroyed them."

"Good! Call Sammy, your boss. Tell him you need to be off tomorrow. We'll ride the bike over." She frowned. "Why are you so anxious to buy a car?"

"I'm going out to Mineola this weekend. To see Pop."

"No!" Her voice was wild, slightly desperate. "You can't!"

"Why can't I?" I sounded to myself like a little boy.

"I'm going to invite some of the group in Saturday night. You have to be here."

"Why? They're all *your* friends. They won't miss me."

"Yes they will. They like you."

I did a quick inventory of Fishbein's friends. No, followers. The giant homosexual, Bruno, seemed to like me but fortunately at a platonic level. Beautiful, blond Hal Materno liked me, unfortunately in a romantic sense. Pretty, black Rebecca seemed fond of me; at least she always kissed me. Tit-Tat and Sterling and Jo-Jo and a few forgettable were always at least civil toward me.

There had been a number of subsequent parties either at the Higgins' apartment, Fishbein's or other foul Astoria lairs, but all had been so similar to the initial gathering, I have spared mention of them. Frankly I found them mildly boring and slightly spooky—Fishbein ruling, but never touched or touching. Now she was trying to control me. And I was allowing it to happen.

I compromised. "Well, I'll just run out there for the day on Saturday."

She looked at me thoughtfully, then nodded her acquiescence. "Go call Sammy. About tomorrow."

* * * *

If anyone is of faint heart respective to motorcycling, I do not suggest a seventy-mile-an-hour ride across the Tappan Zee Bridge. I willed myself to grasp the small of Fishbein's hour-glass tightly and to look neither right nor left nor up nor down, but still nausea washed through my gut until we were past the Hudson River. On the other hand, if you are going used car shopping, a Fishbein in your corner is a definite plus. In a handful of caustic words, she drained away any glibness and shattered the confident veneer of salesmen.

We visited lot after lot. Once I spied a blue Oldsmobile which seemed as though it ought to be within my price range. The salesman said assuredly, "This was taken in trade from a wealthy local woman."

Fishbein snorted derisively and declared, "If she was wealthy it is because of marriage or inheritance. Before that she used this fucking beast as a taxi in the Bronx." Putting her boot on the bumper, she bored into the man, "Admit it. What color was this thing before you had it painted? A shitty paint job at that. And if you think I believe that 51,000 miles, you still must have wet dreams. This is a wreck! You got a decent car on the lot?"

Then I spotted just what I wanted—a four-year-old Ford Maverick coupe. Just an ordinary car with a gearshift. It wasn't dented or rusty, but the paint, originally, I supposed, a lime metallic, had faded to a mottled army green. It suggested the less than thirty thousand miles on the odometer was correct.

Fishbein assailed the unctuous salesman, "Look, is that piece of shit any good? Does it run?"

"Oh, perfectly, madam."

"Do not call me 'madam.' I don't run a whorehouse."

"Of course." He was flustered. "I mean, of course not. Mr. Flanders routinely trades his cars here every four years. Has them serviced by the book. It's an excellent value at one thousand ninety-five dollars."

"Humph. I'll try it out." She then put the car through suicidal antics that surely Mr. Flanders, or even the manufacturer, would never have considered and proclaimed the car satisfactory, by a quick, conspiratorial wink to me.

"How much again?"

"One thousand ninety-five dollars and it's a firm price," he said.

"Don't shit me. 'Firm price' is not in a car dealer's vocabulary. I'll give you nine-fifty and tax."

The man looked furtively hesitant. "I'm not sure. I'll have to ask the manager."

"Fine. You do that. But you better ask him before we walk across this lot. After that, put us in your fucking life history."

If there was a ruling managerial authority, he agreed quickly to our—Fishbein's—offer. "Yes!" He called shrilly to our vanishing backs. "It's a deal!"

I handed over the money from the insurance check I'd cashed at the branch of Chemical Bank wondering for the thousandth time how that financial institution had come to choose its name. Fishbein paid the difference, saving me from a return trip across the Tappan Zee as a passenger on the Harley. It was worth every penny of the nine hundred fifty dollars plus tax.

*****

Pop characteristically answered on the first ring. It was his way of showing how anxious he was to talk to whomever might be calling. He was always pleasant to people even if they were attempting to sell items he had no intention of purchasing or soliciting donations for charities he did not support. His standard jovial repulsion was, "But if I send that money to you, I won't be able to pay my telephone bill and then you won't be able to call me again."

"Hi, Pop. You have anything planned for tomorrow? Thought I'd run out for the day."

"Sure. Why not for the weekend?"

"Sorry. Can't. I'm guest of honor at a party tomorrow night."

"Are you bringing your girlfriend?"

"No."

"You two haven't had a lover's spat, have you?" he asked, trying his level best to purge his voice of any note of hopefulness.

"Nothing like that. She's busy."

Just then Fishbein appeared in the kitchen doorway totally nude, a can of sperm-murdering foam in her hand which she bent over and applied as I watched, creating a viable distraction in my conversation. "I'll be out about nine in the morning."

"Fine, Roy. I'll look forward to it."

Our love-making was always zesty, almost violent, but on that particular mid-October early evening Fishbein demonstrated almost boundless intensity; as though she were playing a fine symphony with our combined bodies. It was so strenuous that in the aftermath I dozed fitfully. Once the ring of the telephone roused me to semi-wakefulness. Then a bark from Fishbein announced in her own subtle way that dinner was served. "You want I should have the butler bring you sustenance, already? Come on!"

Finished with our Franco-American Italian feast, Fishbein brought two more bottles of beer to the table and, after lighting a cigarette, laughed shortly.

"What's funny?"

"A cafe in Brooklyn had a slogan painted in black letters on the white outside wall. It was supposed to read: IF YOUR WIFE CAN'T COOK—EAT HERE, but some witty soul had painted white over the final "E.""

I lit a cigarette, figured it out, then laughed. "Is that a suggestion?"

"If you don't like my Italian cooking. Oh, by the way, Rebecca's going with you tomorrow."

"Rebecca? What on earth for?"

Usually Fishbein made fun of Mother's expression, "What on earth," ingrained into my verbal repertoire, but that evening she ignored it. "She likes you. Wants to meet your father. But if you're a true-blue racist, she'll probably agree to ride in the back seat."

"I'm no racist. Rebecca is sweet, but I hardly know her. What will I talk about? What will my father talk to her about?"

But I knew, or was sure, that Rebecca was a guard; Fishbein's assurance that I would return to her—that I wouldn't jump ship, desert in action. I glanced at the poster above the sofa and saw not Adolph Hitler but Fishbein, and the young Aryan presumably orally caressing the genitals was no stranger. That was, in fact, me. I felt helpless and, yes, frightened.

"Rebecca is good company."

"All right. Whatever you say. She's pretty, too. Where do I pick her up?"

Fishbein gave an address, quite nearby, and added "She said she would be waiting in front of the apartment building."

"I still don't understand *why*."

"Ask her. It was her idea." She was losing interest in the exchange.

I have previously described Rebecca as being a pretty black girl who smoked dope and was Sterling Higgins' secretary. She was actually quite beautiful, a good conversationalist, apparently well-educated and, I guessed, genuinely liked me. That is, no one else kissed me at Fishbein's instigated parties although Hal Materno may have wished to do so.

In appearance, Rebecca was very dark-skinned but her features—thin lips, narrow, straight nose—made her more a Caucasian girl with an impossibly deep tan.

Her clothes were always tasteful, never flaunting her impressive curves nor apologizing for them.

I thought all these things as I finished the Ethel Waters' chapter, entitled "Am I Blue?" Then I realized that the book was nearly complete, with only the final Lee Wiley bio to write and an epilogue. Fishbein and I had agreed initially that we would profile our subjects in alphabetical order, that any other grouping was potentially tedious and subjective.

Where we had disagreed, when the manuscript was half-completed, was which of our names ought to be listed first. "Why the fuck should Roy Chandler be first?"

"Alphabetical order," I had reasoned.

"Bullshit! I've done all the hard digging while you've sat here typing like a prima donna."

"Surely a fully-liberated woman like yourself is not suggesting ladies before gentlemen."

"Fuck you! We'll let the publisher decide."

"If we find a publisher?"

"Yeah. If." Then we had gone to bed. Not to sleep.

There was so much more I knew about Ethel Waters than I did about Rebecca, but I still found myself comparing the two. At that time, in 1975, Ethel Waters was still living and singing at Billy Graham Crusades, but it had been from roots I suspected were unfamiliar to Rebecca. For Ethel Waters had risen from beginnings in the ghetto of Chester, Pennsylvania—euphemistically a suburb of Philadelphia. Born in 1896, she was surrounded by all the squalor and privation which was the lot of most black people of her era, including Billie Holiday, whom Rebecca could so expertly imitate.

According to Rebecca, she had been raised in Bergenfield, New Jersey and her father was an independent businessman. Her mother was a music teacher. No, blacks didn't enjoy complete equality but matters were certainly improving for them.

As I finished typing, the exclamation, "Shit!" drifted to my ears from the bathroom.

"That's what one frequently encounters in that chamber."

"Very funny. It's worse. My period."

"We've lived through several of those before, my dear. In fact, some of your imaginative substitutions have been nearly as satisfying as the real thing."

"Fuck yourself! Selfish male pig!"

* * * *

Rebecca stood on the sidewalk looking handsome in a pale blue suit with a pleated skirt, a red raincoat over her shoulders against the overcast chill autumn morning. She opened the car door and hesitated, "Roy? Where do I sit?"

"How about on your ass?"

"I mean...Fishbein said you were such a terrible bigot you might make me sit in the back seat."

"Fishbein is full of shit. You sit right next to me. Even snuggle up on my shoulder if you want to."

To my surprise she did just that, kissed me and said, "Good morning." She smelled like spice. "How do you like your new car?"

"It's all right. Just doesn't have the personality of the old VW. Maybe it will develop one." I swerved to avoid a vicious pockmark in the pavement.

"I had a Volkswagen. A convertible. Daddy bought it for me when I was in high school."

"What does your father do? You told me once that he was in business for himself."

"He owns franchises for water softeners and supplies. When I was a little girl I wondered why people didn't just not turn on the faucet hard if they wanted soft water." She paused and frowned. "Do you think your father will mind? About me, I mean?"

"Why should he? He's always been nice to my friends."

"Come on, Roy. Be honest. Have you ever brought a nigger home before?"

I laughed. "Relax. Pop likes everyone. If a cat burglar broke into his house, he'd go his bail." Then I asked impulsively, suddenly, "Why don't you look black? I mean, your features. You look almost Polynesian."

"I don't know. All the women on my mother's side of the family have the same looks. Once, my mother tried to do some genealogical research. Despite what Alex Haley has recently claimed in his *Roots* business—which I'm convinced was largely a vivid imagination rather than hard facts—information about black people's heritage is severely limited. The best my mother could find out was that her great-great-grandfather in Virginia had bought his freedom from a man named Chandler. Say, Roy, you don't suppose?"

"That your however many great-grandfathers once was owned by my family?" I shook my head. "Not a chance. All my family settled and stayed in New York and Vermont. But they did own slaves. Just as domestic servants. Back in the days when my family had money. Days, by the way, that I don't remember."

"About being Polynesian: when I was a little girl, I used to claim I was from Hawaii. Some asinine liberal teacher even put it on my school records. By the time I was in high school, I regretted it. The black kids thought I was putting on airs and the white kids just laughed; thought I was a fake. No, I'm just a black girl. Don't think anything else."

"Where did you go to college?"

"My BA is from Oberlin in Ohio. My Master's in Public Administration is from Columbia. So, I'm secretary to Sterling who barely has a Bachelor's in Art History from City University."

"You resent him? His job?"

"No. He was there first. I'm glad to have a job and be able to be on my own. I wouldn't want the city to switch our jobs, whatever my qualifications are. Now, I would be pissed off if Sterling got a promotion and they hired an art history major—black or white—to be my new boss. All blacks aren't hung up on being oppressed. I'm not, anyway."

"I'm glad. Why did you want to come with me today?"

"Fishbein told me to." She looked surprised. "I'm not a prisoner of the city. I like to get out."

"Are you a slave to Fishbein?"

She hesitated. "No. I don't think so. Are you?"

"I don't know," I said, turning on the windshield wipers because it had begun to drizzle. We traveled the remainder of the time in troubled silence.

*****

Leaves were grudgingly being raked as I turned in to the driveway in Mineola. It occurred to me that my father was becoming increasingly fastidious about caring for his house. In the days of my tenancy, he either paid me fifty cents to rake the leaves or they stayed in the yard, much to Mother's displeasure.

Since once again the car was unfamiliar, and at least one of the occupants was black, he only gave a cursory glance at us, not breaking the rhythm of his raking. Arthur Avenue ran a total of six blocks and it always seemed as though a disproportionate number of cars turning around chose that particular driveway. But when I switched off the ignition he paused. He then recognized me and grinned, dropping the rake in the leaf pile.

Rebecca emerged looking timid. Pop said: "Well, hello, young lady. Roy said he was coming alone. I'm glad he changed his mind."

I introduced Rebecca and he shook her hand firmly, displaying not a trace of racial rancor. "Come in! I'll make coffee. How's the book coming, Roy?"

"One more chapter; then the hard part, finding a publisher."

"What do you do, Rebecca?"

"I work for the city. I'm a secretary."

"How interesting."

She smiled showing her dimples and dazzling, white, even teeth. "It isn't. It's boring as hell."

Pop laughed and held up his hands. "All right. I'll just make coffee. My secretary would say the same thing."

Pop overdid being tolerant. Once we were seated he said ecstatically, "I can't believe this girl is black! She has the most beautiful features!"

Rebecca was equally tolerant. "Well, I am black. I assure you Roy and I are just friends."

It could have been a difficult day, but it wasn't.

We were served a lunch of fish stew which Pop insisted Rebecca wouldn't like, but which, in fact, she did—asking for and eating a second helping. She then asked if she could take a nap. He provided his own bedroom, asking solicitously if it was warm enough, then rejoined me in the kitchen for coffee.

"You look upset, Pop. What's wrong? Rebecca?"

He shook his head. "A young woman came here last night. She asked how she could get in touch with you. Of course, I don't know anything about your social life. I didn't want to give her the telephone number in Queens."

My father used the terms social life and sex life synonymously and was obviously in fear that I was about to be named in a paternity suit. And I was thankful he hadn't given whomever it was Fishbein's number.

"Did she give her name?"

"Yes. And she left a card. Asked me to have you call her if I heard from you anytime soon."

"What was her name? It wasn't Sally Becker, was it?"

"No, nothing like that. Catherine Archer, maybe? I'll get the card." He went into the living room, fumbled in the clutter on the coffee table and returned, handing me the card without comment.

It was buff colored and thick with shiny, embossed, gold block letters which read:

Interiors by Christine

Complete interior decoration

It displayed the name Christine Arthur, Designer, and an address and telephone number in Annandale, Virginia. Handwritten in the corner was a local telephone number.

"I'll be damned," I said in awe, "Christine. After all these years. I'll go call her."

"Who is she?"

"Don't you remember? Christine was the girl I went with that summer I spent with you right after high school."

He shook his head. "I recall you went out almost every evening. I assumed you had dates, but I didn't realize it was always the same girl. Sorry."

"Don't be sorry. It was just a summer fling. I'm just surprised she wants to get in touch now. Really, I'm amazed she isn't married."

"Maybe she is. Nowadays a lot of women use their maiden names, especially in business."

"Pop, women who are married don't usually try to contact men they've…" I broke off, somewhat embarrassed.

"Slept with?" he prompted.

"More or less, but if you've ever knocked off a piece inside a Volkswagen, you sure as hell wouldn't say 'slept.'"

Pop laughed. "I've never tried."

As I walked to the telephone in the guest bedroom—my bedroom—I reflected on that summer and it occurred to me that I had never brought Christine to meet my father any more than she had thought of introducing me to her grandfather. We were both too wrapped up in the give and take of carnal pleasure to consider social niceties. How simple and innocent that affair had been compared to the complex and possibly threatening relationship in which I was embroiled with Fishbein.

*****

"Arthur residence," came the still remembered lilting tones of Christine's voice.

"Christine! This is Roy Chandler. How are you?"

"Well, well, I must say you're more prompt at returning telephone calls than answering letters." Her voice was, I believe the word is, tart.

"Letters? You wrote me a letter?"

"*A* letter. I wrote you fifty! A hundred! Good God, Roy! Maybe a *thousand* letters! Some I sent to City Island. Some to your address here."

"I'm sorry, Christine. I never got a letter from you." Then I saw a flash of Fishbein examining the forwarded envelopes the week before. God! Mother! I asked evenly, "What did you write in your letters?"

"About school. Rehashing our romance. Some was a little juicy, to pique your remembering me. Why? You're not going to try to tell me someone censored your mail?"

"I've only very recently learned that that is the case. I'm sorry. I apologize for my mother as well. I can't make you believe me, but it's true."

"Are you married, Roy?"

"No."

"Engaged?"

"No."

"Having an affair?"

"I'm beginning to think the affair is having me. How about you?"

"None of the above. I've had affairs, but none which are remarkable. Are you free tonight?"

"I wish I was. I'm just here for the day and I have a friend with me, or I'd run over now. Are you just here for the weekend?"

"No. I'll be here for about a month, maybe six weeks."

"How can you? Don't you have a business? Live in Virginia? See? I read your card."

She laughed. "My business will have to go to the dogs for now. I'm here to settle Grandfather's estate. He died last week."

"Oh. I'm sorry."

"Don't be. He was ninety-one, died in his sleep. And for the last ten years he was an unspeakable old grouch. On the other hand, he left all his money to me." She paused. "So tell me. How is the current lover? As good as I was?"

"God, Christine! That's like comparing the sinking of the "Titanic" with a crashed airliner."

"That may not be a compliment."

"It isn't one to me. I was the captain and could be the pilot. I ought to have been or should be in better control."

"Go ahead, Roy. Be a masochist. Sometimes things are beyond your control. Like with your mother, if that's to be believed."

"It is, but..." I burst out in spontaneous and uncontrollable laughter.

"What's so damn funny?"

"I know you better after five minutes on the phone than in a whole summer years ago. Can I call you? Next time I come out?"

"Sure, Roy. I'd like that."

I wandered back to the kitchen with mixed feelings of anger and regret. My mother had deceived me but I couldn't disregard her protective maternal instincts even if they had wronged me. What angered me most was that she was still doing the wrong.

"Pop?" I asked quietly.

He looked up, arching his eyebrows inquiringly.

"When I was in college, did I ever get any mail sent to your address?"

"Sure, quite a lot. I just forwarded it all to you at City Island. It made sense. If you'll recall it was sometimes a month or more between your visits by then."

"You don't remember any from Christine Arthur?"

He shook his head. "It seems to me there were a lot with an upstate address. Ithaca maybe? I usually didn't look, just wrote, 'Please forward.'"

"Hmm" That made sense. Pop was uninquisitive and

Christine had gone to Cornell.

"Is it important?"

"No. I guess not. It might have been at one time." I poured some more coffee. "All right, Pop. I haven't seen you since Sag Harbor. What did you think of Fishbein?"

He smiled. "I've forgotten the exact wording of your initial description, but it was deadly accurate. I was impressed, I guess. Your Aunt Sylvia summed it up astutely."

"What did she say?"

"'If he marries her, he'll never need to buy a Doberman Pincer.'"

I laughed, then said musingly, "Marry."

"Do you want to marry her?"

"I'm not sure, but I'll tell you one thing: there will be no grandchildren to bounce on your knee."

"Why not?"

"Fishbein made it clear, early in our relationship, that she refused to ever have children."

"Why?"

"Let's just say she had an unhappy childhood."

"But..." Pop shrugged. "It's your life. I can't make your decisions for you."

"I wish someone—someone other than Mother—would."

Then Rebecca came sleepily into the room and any chances of confidential talk was ended. She said, "I slept two hours! That was rude of me." Smiling slyly, she quipped, "I'll be providing credence to the belief that black people are lazy."

"Nonsense!" my father said heartily. "I'm glad you thought my bed was comfortable."

The balance of the afternoon was taken up in a discussion that basically served to establish that black middle-class youth in New Jersey evolved to adulthood in much the same way as their white counterparts on Long Island.

That night, at Fishbein's party, I got drunk. This was not a remarkable experience for me. I was drained emotionally, having finished, "Easy to Love" the Lee Wiley chapter even as the noise of Fishbein's compatriots began and sickly-sweet marijuana smoke filled the apartment. The book was essentially finished! So I drank to its completion and collapsed in bed at some indeterminate point.

During the night, silence suggesting that the party had concluded, I roused to the banging of the steam heat system in the old building and found that I was naked. Did I take my clothes off? I couldn't remember. A dexterous hand was rubbing my chest coming ever closer to and then encircling my swelling penis. I reached over and stroked Fishbein's breasts. The nipples didn't seem as large. Moving my hand down to her crotch, where the hair didn't seem as dense but was more wiry, I sought out her mouth to kiss her and when I did the odor of cinnamon touched my nostrils and when our lips met I put my arm on her warm velvety back and recoiled. It wasn't Fishbein! I raised up on my elbow, now fully wakeful, and studied my bed-mate in the dimness. "Rebecca! What in hell are you doing here?"

"Waiting for you to fuck me, Roy."

"Where is Fishbein? She'll kill you!"

"She isn't here."

"That's obvious."

"Don't you want to?"

"That's beside the point."

She cradled my genitals in both hands, kissed me long and hard then whispered, "*I'm* beside the point. Come on!"

So I did and it was good. I refused to compare her with my usual bed partner, but Rebecca was splendid. I lay atop of her several minutes after we were both satisfied. She said quietly, "God, I wanted that. You. Can you do it again!"

A rasping noise sounded in the corner, then a flare of light and, quickly looking up, I saw the round orange glow of a cigarette tip. "Don't be greedy, Rebecca," Fishbein said sharply, "I said you could have him once. Just once."

Fury grasped me. I leaped out of the bed and confronted Fishbein. "*You said!* What the fuck gives you the right to say who can have me? I am *not* a male whore! You are *not* my pimp! You understand?"

"Didn't you enjoy it?" she asked mildly.

"That's got nothing to do with it. *Why* did you do it?" My headache was making me nauseous and I felt a little foolish standing there naked, with a deflated organ, yelling at her.

Rebecca sat up in bed and said, "It's because I'm in love with you, Roy."

"That's the reason, Chandler. I thought it was easier to let her have you one time than compete with her." Her tone was highly logical.

"That is my fucking decision, Fishbein. Understand?" I retrieved my briefs, snatched the blanket from the bed and stalked into the living room where I resettled on the sofa, still nauseated, still angry, able to hear Fishbein and Rebecca in quiet conversation until I fell asleep allowing my body to complete metabolizing the excess of alcohol I'd inflicted upon it.

At some point during the mid-morning, I began to awaken,

a heavy weight upon my chest. Doing a quick self-diagnosis, I decided that too many beers and Marlboros were at fault. But, then, why was my chest wet and the weight moving? I chanced opening my eyes a chink. Fishbein was kneeling on the floor, her head on my chest. She had apparently been crying so long her face was red and swollen, almost unpretty.

Sensing that I was gaining consciousness, she cried out between sobs, "Oh, Chandler!…I'm sorry…I warned you…that I didn't know…about love!"

Not feeling healthy enough to rehash events of the night before, I asked weakly, "Is there any coffee?"

"Yeah. I'll get you a cup."

"Get my cigarettes, too, will you?"

"Where are they?"

"I think on the bureau in the bedroom, but I may be having memory lapses."

"Tied one on last night, huh?"

"Yeah. And last night, too," I said, but she was gone. I decided to try a glimpse of the world, and sat up, slowly, painfully. I may live, I thought weakly.

Coffee in a chipped cup and a battered Marlboro pack appeared on the table thanks to Fishbein the contrite.

"Are you going to haul ass, now? Jump ship."

"There's a book to finish. Then…" I shrugged.

She looked at me sadly. "I love you, Chandler. That's the reason I do so many crazy things. I don't want you should get bored with me."

"I promise there's never a dull moment."

Her eyes filled with tears, both of her hands gripped my right arm—fortunately I had set down the scalding coffee. "Chandler," she said urgently, "Do you know what I did when I found my old lady dead?"

Clearly I couldn't have known. I shook my head.

"I started kicking her! Over and over. Then so hard she rolled over. I expected her eyes to be open, but so was her mouth. She didn't have a tongue! The stuff she drank had dissolved her tongue!"

"God! Fishbein, my stomach is a little weak. Is there a point to what you're telling me?"

"Of course. When you've hated as much as I have, it's hard to know how to love. You understand?"

"I guess. Right now I need fresh air. I'm going for a walk."

"Just a walk?"

"I'm not running out on you, Fishbein," I told her darkly. She kissed me and smiled.

* * * *

For some reason, unbeknown to me to this day, I was drawn to walk the six blocks to Rebecca's apartment building. Perhaps I wanted to see her in the raw light of the day, demand an explanation of the previous night's intrusion. Conversely, it was possible I was attracted to Rebecca, but had not realized it before.

Her building was marginally newer and better maintained than Fishbein's. In the lobby—this was hardly a doorman-staffed establishment—I looked at the bank of brushed aluminum mailboxes and located...nothing! I didn't even know her last name! There was an R. Albritton and an R. S. Brown, plus an R. Yarusi which I dismissed immediately. In fact, I dismissed Rebecca. Again I felt used and dirty, a unwitting participant in a gangbang. I walked back home, that was, to Fishbein's. I didn't suppose I had any other home.

When I released the door locks, the apartment was a scene of action. Chapters of the manuscript were everywhere, red pen markings and question marks galore. Fishbein herself was on the telephone in the kitchen, I could hear her staccato voice, "Listen, this is straight manuscript typing. Not poetry. Chicago style. An inch of margin all around. Easy. Fifty cents a page is a gift."

I gathered acquiescence.

"The catch is the deadline is Wednesday."

Protestation.

"Bullshit! You know fucking well you can do it."

Negotiation.

"Yeah. All right. I can fix it. I'll deliver the manuscript first thing tomorrow. Pay in advance? You're shitting me. On delivery and it better be perfect."

Fishbein came into the living room flushed, the dark eyes flashing, dressed in worn jeans, a see-through sweater and—seeing through—no bra. "We got to work fast, Chandler. I got our finish typing set up. Let's do final editing. Can you arrange a meeting with Zuma Alcorn? For tonight? I know of an editor who—assuming he likes it—will treat this as a labor of love, furnish photos, the works!"

"I'll call her. But why?"

"See these question marks? She may be able to verify facts that are only educated guesses to us."

"What if she can't?"

"No problem. We put in disclaimers like, 'It is believed' or 'many have said' and let it ride. We're not claiming to be ultimate historical authorities. Besides, half our subjects are dead. Who's to complain? Those still alive and lucid would be hard-pressed to remember themselves. You didn't intend this to be a definitive history, did you?"

"No, but I've tried to make it as accurate as possible."

"Good. That's what I want it should be, too. By the way, you got a loose hundred? I'm nearly broke until I get my next royalty check on the first of the month."

I did. My checking account had burgeoned to over six hundred dollars, so I had just cashed Sammy's payroll check on Friday. Cohabiting may have been immoral but it certainly helped financially. Nevertheless I asked, "Why don't we just type it ourselves? Save some money?"

"We want it to look professional. My typewriter is good, yours is a little better. We want polish! See what I mean? And time. I could finish type a chapter in a week. I'd guess you could do about the same. That's three months we're talking. I want fast action, don't you?"

"All right. I've got the cash. Let's get busy."

*****

It rained most of the afternoon, turned cold with the darkness, and the streets were shiny with ice. Glancing out the window, Fishbein observed, "Jesus, the driving is going to be murder. We'll take the Plymouth tonight. It's heavier and I won't shed a tear if it gets a few more dents."

Few cars and fewer pedestrians were out as Fishbein cautiously drove to Kew Gardens. "God, Chandler, this is like glass! I hope no one does anything stupid."

Someone did. In front of a well-lighted tavern, a man threw open the door of a newish Buick. Fishbein tried to brake but the car began to skid. "Fuck it!" she said breathlessly and came out of the spin with the Buick's door briefly on her hood. Then it clattered onto the payment. I looked behind us. The man was gazing incredulously at his car door.

"Aren't you going to stop?"

"What for?"

"Isn't that a 'hit and run' or something?"

"You see any witnesses?"

"No."

"Not even him. Besides, he's not going to call the fuzz. Would you if you were coming out of a bar? Probably near drunk? Besides, I'm probably doing the guy a favor."

"Why?"

"If it's a hit and run, on his insurance, he files on his comprehensive which has a lower deductible than his collision. Now, don't bother me. This kind of driving requires concentration."

*****

Zuma Alcorn seemed overjoyed that we had come. "I was afraid you wouldn't chance it. That ice looks hellish. Did you have any problems?"

"None worth mentioning," Fishbein said smoothly.

"Well, I'm delighted you're here. I'm not above drinking alone, but I prefer company and I'm too damn old for after-theater party antics. That's for the kids."

In the kitchen, out of Fishbein's earshot she said, "Roy, it's none of my business, but I think you ought to call your mother. She's concerned about you."

"Concerned about the evil of my ways? No thanks. I've heard her dissertation on her reprobate son."

"I think you'll find she's changed. Your moving out rattled her, but it also made her realize you're a young man now, in charge of your own life. She may not like your living arrangement, but she still loves you."

"I suppose she does." Then in a flash I realized how alike and limited Fishbein and Mother were in their ability to love. Mother had always doled out her love judiciously and methodically, never spontaneously, as though to love too much was like putting too many pharmaceuticals in a client's portfolio. Clandestinely reading and censoring my mail was and had been her way of reading me as though I were an IRS audit or the *New York Times* financial pages.

There was Fishbein, who had so long been unloved and unwilling to love, now trying desperately to learn and thus far had only mastered the physical aspects.

I likened her to a formerly wild mare, continually in heat, but suspicious of anyone's motives who might offer her a sugar lump and was still not, perhaps never would be, saddle-broken. In other words, her ability to love spiritually was as primitive as an early adolescent. But she was trying. In that instant, I felt pity for both of them.

Zuma Alcorn paused, greedily snatched a Marlboro from my pack, which I had come to automatically remove from my pocket and place on the coffee table upon our arrivals, and blissfully lit it. Then she said wistfully, "I hope when this wrap-up session is concluded tonight you two won't stop coming by. I've come to depend on them to keep my mind—I think the word is—honed. Also feeling young."

"*I* won't stop," Fishbein said firmly, as if she assumed that I would.

"I won't either," I said quickly, defensively.

And neither of us ever did forget, not even until the week before Zuma Alcorn was killed over twelve years later.

*****

Returning home—or to the Astoria apartment—Fishbein only spoke once, and it was through a sheen of tears. She said quietly, composedly, "So we're all finished, Chandler, huh?"

"With this. There could be a sequel if this is a success. Like *Three Little Words,* but feature men, or couples."

She nodded slowly and returned her attention to the treacherous streets. No more car doors that night.

21

The book sold! That is, it found an enthusiastic editor, Allen Klein of Biograph Books. Fishbein threw herself upon me as I came into the apartment on a Monday in early November. "We've got it placed, Chandler!"

"I haven't placed it in. Not yet. Must be someone else's."

"The book, asshole! We've done it! I just got off the phone with the editor. He loves it! It's a labor of love for him. I told you he'd go for it! Plus he's got all kinds of photographs of his own that he wants to plug in. He plans a slick book, $24.95 retail cover!"

"Hold on! What terms?"

"Five thousand advance. Sliding royalties on gross from seven up to twelve percent."

"Twenty-five hundred each?"

"Up front, yeah. But Klein is going to *push* it. Take my word for it. The contract is being typed as we speak. There's one downside, though."

"Usually there is. What is it?"

"She seemed to be choosing her words carefully. "It seems he has a problem with the title. He considered it too trite and that it called attention away from the subject matter."

"He has a better idea?"

"Yeah. He wants to call it *Singing Sweethearts.*"

"Talk about trite."

In tribute to our elevated status, Fishbein threw a monumental bohemian bash on Thursday night. It would turn out to be our last night of cohabitation. Early in the evening, prior to the arrival of the gang, I impulsively decided to call Mother.

"Well, my goodness, Roy! So nice of you to call. There isn't anything wrong, is there?"

"Not that I know of. I just haven't talked to you in a while. Thought I'd see how you're doing." What an absolutely worthless conversation, I thought.

"Oh, just fine. Work at the office has been quite heavy. How are you and your...your friend coming along on your book?"

"Fishbein," I reminded her.

"Yes. Right. Well!" She wasn't going to utter the name.

"The book's finished. We even have a publisher."

"How wonderful! Will you be coming home?"

Home. Now precisely where was that? City Island? Or Astoria? Or Mineola? Or, hell, the interior of my tidy Ford Maverick. "I'm not sure. I'll let you know."

Silence. Then, "Right, let me know what you decide. You're always welcome here, Roy."

"Thanks, Mother. Good night." I hung up quickly, relieved.

Also, before the first guest arrived Fishbein and I made love, she with unprecedented abandon and forcefulness; I tentatively, as though I were a virgin. It would be our last coupling.

We sat up in bed naked, smoking, initially silent. Finally she asked, "Was it good? To you?"

"Great."

"It hasn't been the same. Not since Rebecca." Her voice was quiet, matter of fact.

"No, I guess it hasn't."

"Why? Was she better than me?"

"No, Fishbein. It's just that I've felt used—even abused—

since that night."

She turned to face me. "What's that supposed to mean?"

"Just what I said. You can love me. You can do business with me. You can fuck me. But you cannot, repeat, cannot control me—or abuse me."

"I see. So you're feeling a little of what I lived through. What I still live through."

"No, Fishbein, I could never even picture those degraded parts of your life. I can just tell you it's best for you to put them behind you."

She said nothing for a time. Then, "Roy?"

Never had she uttered my first name. I glanced at her. "What?"

"I've loved you the hardest I know how. Do you know that?"

"I know." And I did know.

"Now, let's get ready. Party time is at hand!"

But she didn't sound happy, nor did I feel it.

* * * *

Nor was it a festive evening despite all the superficial hilarity and usual beer and dope and music. There was, beneath the veneer of conviviality, an odd tension, even hostility. I mentioned this to Fishbein, but she gave a dismissive flick of her wrist and said, "Shit. They're just jealous of us. Our success." Then she hurried away to where Jo-Jo was guiding a vacuous blond woman toward her—our—bedroom. "Not a chance, Jo-Jo. You're not fucking her on *my* bed, messing up the goddam sheets. Take her down to the basement or somewhere."

I didn't know the blond's name, nor had I known the names of any of his previous dates—if that word isn't too staid a name for the various women of the moment—nor, I suspected, did Jo-Jo. They were just vacant vaginas that he occupied in passing. I pictured his relationships as checking into empty available motel rooms of sexual pleasure as he carried on in his trade as, say, a salesman of sexual novelties traveling about peddling his wares to pornography stores.

Bruno and Materno seemed to be having the homosexual equivalent of a lover's spat, resulting in Bruno's stalking out of the apartment alone, a surly expression on his face. I did not know nor have I ever learned the emotional make-up of those who engage in deviant sexual behavior. Yes, I repeat, deviant. What I, to this day, consider perverse and repugnant sexual behaviors I am convinced are learned, not inborn. I do not believe anyone was ever born a homosexual, as some persons have blue eyes and others brown. So-called "gay" people are not going to like me or this book, assuming they haven't all killed each other, and maybe, indirectly, many of the rest of us with AIDS. So be it. I offer as an example, one Joseph Oliver Wendell Holmes, known to me only as Jo-Jo. The next and only time I subsequently heard about that individual was in a newspaper article some years later which displayed a picture of him. That was how I came to know his full name. It seems he was arrested in Oswego, New York, for multiple counts of "crimes against nature" for screwing poor, innocent sheep and, God forbid, charging people money to watch him do it! I personally thought the paying voyeurs ought to have been charged with something as well. I ventured this opinion to my wife, who just said, "Oh, Roy. They were enjoying their Constitutional rights; you know, their right to peaceful assembly."

"Oh, yeah? And Jo-Jo was expressing his First Amendment rights. Self-expression?" I countered. But that night in November of 1975 in Astoria, Rebecca and Fishbein were at odds over something unknown to me. At one point, shortly before her early departure, Rebecca sat next to me nearly in tears and said, "She'll barely speak to me, Roy. What's wrong? What have I done?"

"No idea."

"Do you wish you hadn't done it with me?"

"I wish it hadn't been engineered."

"I'm sorry. But that wasn't my idea. I just wanted...you. I still do." Her voice had turned bitter. She handed me a card. It read: "Rebecca C. Albritton" and in black print her address and telephone number. "Call me sometime. It doesn't have to be sex. We could just have lunch." Then she kissed me in that way of hers that no woman before or since has been able to duplicate, like my stomach was imploding. And she was gone.

I did call Rebecca, as she had asked, and I see her almost every night, have for years. No, not as a wife or lover although she is just as exquisite as ever. She is now—has been for a number of years—the chief information official for the City of New York. I see her almost nightly on the television news describing with equal aplomb the city's stance on bludgeonings to building projects.

Only Tit-Tat and Sterling seemed their usual selves, as did the hangers-on whose names, if I ever knew them, I've long since forgotten. As a buffer to the disharmony in my surroundings, I got drunker than I had ever been in my life. No mean achievement.

When I awoke, or at least rose to a semi-comatose state, I opened my eyes just a chink. Daylight. Worse yet morning sunlight. I closed them painfully and assessed the condition of my self-ravaged body. That's the problem with a hangover—it's so difficult to blame it on anyone else. My head was pounding relentlessly, my breath passed through a gritty desert of a mouth foul with stale booze and my right forearm was asleep from having collapsed on it. I was a mess.

Geographically, I decided I was on the living room sofa, and clad only in my Hanes briefs. Whether I or someone else had undressed me, was not within recollection. Then, my underpants were snatched off of me, arms encircled my waist and a wet tongue and mouth went to work on my genitals. I thought,

Fishbein, you pick the worst times. Painfully opening my eyes I focused on the smiling upside-down face of Fishbein, her blouse unbuttoned, her breasts bare. She put her hands on my biceps and bent her breasts toward my face.

Now wait! If she was at that end of the sofa, then who?... Surely not Rebecca again! Searing pain as my head jolted up. God! Far worse! It was the fag, Hal Materno, plying his arts. I could have kicked him away. I could have pushed Fishbein off of me. Instead I was mesmerized with horror, partly because I was fully erect, responding to his no doubt extensive skills.

Fishbein lowered her breasts to my forehead. I willed myself to thoughts that would return me to a state of flaccidity. Mother, Pop, Sammy Shinbaum, the collie I'd once seen struck by an automobile on the Expressway, mortally injured but still valiantly struggling to rise. Nothing was working and momentarily I climaxed; heard him gulping. "Beautiful," he said withdrawing.

"I'm glad I wasn't sleeping on my stomach," was all I could croak.

"Some other time" he said breezily.

"*No* other time, Materno!" Fishbein warned too loudly for my aching head. "I told you just once, as a favor."

I returned to the cocoon of coma, too lethargic and ill to feel anger or revulsion or shame. That would come.

It couldn't have been long until I decided to brave the relative comforts of inertness. I sat up. Fishbein bustled into the room, the white blouse now fastened over a bra with a pleated maroon skirt and black heels. In her hand was a cup of coffee which she placed before me while she gave an appraising look. "Christ, Chandler! You look like the wrath of God and that is something coming from an atheist."

I sipped the coffee, spied my shirt on the coffee table and got my cigarette pack. "I don't exactly feel like Superman, or even Clark Kent."

She got down on her knees in front of me and lit my cigarette for me. I remembered her in that same position and place saying, "I want we should be lovers." But this time, after I had exhaled, she kissed me briefly and said, "I have to go downtown. Meeting with our editor."

"You're going to handle everything?"

"I don't think you're in any shape to tag along. Besides you told me you didn't know shit about the business end. We still split fifty-fifty."

"Fine." I finished my cigarette and coffee before asking the question she was waiting to answer. "Why did you do it?"

"Materno adores you and...and then it was part of the deal."

"What deal?"

"That he'd type the manuscript in three days. He's the one who typed it."

"Jesus! Who have you got lined up for me next? A gorilla from the Bronx Zoo? And is it male or female?" I didn't feel healthy enough to yell.

"There won't be another one," she said firmly.

"That's a fucking relief."

"Chandler." That soft tone she had used in that same place and position months earlier when she had told me she wanted me to touch her bare breasts and I had. "I warned you I didn't know about love, that I might make mistakes, that you were the only man I'd ever wanted to teach me. I'm sorry for the crazy things I've done." Her eyes were moist. Abruptly she kissed me and rose to her feet. "Christ, Chandler! You need to brush your teeth! And I've got to go. I'll be late." She picked up her camel's hair overcoat and at the door, just before she closed it behind her, she said quietly, "Goodbye, Roy."

Fishbein stood outside the door for two minutes, perhaps in indecision, then I heard the click of her heels on the floor of the hallway and down the stairs. And when they were no longer audible I knew what I had to do. Leave! Not just the apartment. Not just Fishbein. Everything! I had to start a life, one in which *I* was in control.

When Fishbein had said, "Goodbye, Roy," she was giving me the greatest tribute to her love for me of which she was capable— freedom. Maybe she had an appointment with the editor, perhaps not. Her absence signified she had leashed her guard dogs, cut the power to the high voltage fence. I was free! And in that moment of insightfulness I loved her more than I ever had in bed.

Quickly I shaved, then showered, giving special attention to my privates to purge them of their recent debasement and dressed in the best outfit I owned. While I drank more coffee and smoked, I wrote a note. It said:

> *Fishbein:*
> *Please forward all mail to me*
> *c/o Mrs. Helen Chandler*
> *#18 Brandt Place*
> *New...*

I stopped writing. Wrong place. I looked about the shabby

apartment. There was more here, in just a few months' time, that was familiar and dear to me, than in years of living in the City Island house. Glancing at my watch, I saw it was ten o'clock. There was something painful I had to do. I shredded my note and dialed the Bronx number for Shinbaum's Kosher Meats.

"You got problems, Roy?"

"Yeah, Sammy. I'm giving you my two weeks' notice."

"Whatsamatta? You want a raise?"

"No. You're paying me too much now. I need a change. For everything to be different."

"Oh. That's the case, you can't give me notice. I'm layin' ya off. You're guaranteed two week sev-rince. That's the law. Where you want the checks sent to?"

"I can't ask you to do that, Sammy."

"The law. Besides you been a fine goy. The best. For four years." There was a catch in the voice of the tough Jewish Bronx ex-Marine, ex-Japanese POW. "Then you can apply for unemployment, too."

"But that will cost you even more, Sammy."

"So? Whatsa few bucks between fren's? Listen. Did I ever tell ya the one about the goy graduated from NYU?" He had, but I let him continue. "See, he couldn' get a job. So, one day, walkin' down Sebenth Avenue, a broad says, 'You look good. You wanna blow-job?'

"He says, 'No thanks. I still got three weeks left on my unemployment!'" Laughter roared and I matched it. "Where to send your checks?"

"Twenty-four-sixteen Arthur Avenue, Mineola. And thanks, Sammy."

After hastily packing, I placed the suitcase and garment bag and typewriter in the hall. I wrote a new note to Fishbein providing the Mineola address for forwarding purposes. Then I shut the door and slid the two keys over the threshold. In doing so, I became what is now called a "homeless person." In earlier times the term was "hobo" or "drifter." I have an opinion about that. I think most of the homeless probably have alternate havens or sources of sustenance, but the confines or strictures attached are abhorrent. Many of these people prefer either alcohol or drugs or even uncleanliness to environments which would chain them to intolerable conventions of mind and habit.

So, very briefly, I joined the ranks of the homeless. I tossed my belongings into the trunk of the unscarred, paid for, licensed and insured Maverick, remembered that I had seven hundred ninety-six dollars on deposit at Chemical Bank, whose name origin was and still is a mystery to me, and drove to Manhattan to look for a "decent job." Things weren't all bad.

It was a crisp, clear autumn morning, and as I drove east and then south, dodging potholes and careening taxi-cabs, my spirits soared. I left the car in an attended lot, ate brunch in a crowded luncheonette and hit the pavement. My first target was a giant publishing concern on Fifth Avenue. Might as well start with carriage trade. I wished, seeing the posh lobby, I had not opted to leave my suits and other good clothes at Mother's. I approached the directory board to seek out the floor containing the personnel department.

Despite what Fishbein had accused, I was not entirely ignorant of the machinations of the publishing business. For example, I was aware of the vast distance between an editorial assistant and an assistant editor. The principal difference was money. An assistant editor had an annual income at least one digit longer than the lowly editorial assistant. An editorial assistant was, in fact, simply a copyreader, which was an extraordinarily dull job, but I had to start somewhere.

A shrewd-looking woman who reminded me of Mother asked, "Would you like an application?"

What else? I thought, but said, "Yes, please," and smiled.

Receptionists sometimes had clout. She gestured to a gilt and white French Provincial table and an uncomfortable-looking spindly chair. The questions on the form seemed more concerned with my physical well-being than preparation for the function of reading boring manuscripts. I submitted the completed document to the woman who scanned it cursorily, probably to determine if I was literate, then picked up a telephone and spoke a few hushed words—she could have been calling building security—then suggested I reseat myself. I didn't want to—I was sure I had heard an ominous crack when I sat on the fragile chair the first time—but I gingerly obeyed.

Momentarily a pretty blond woman with an expectant smile on her face, whom I would have asked for a date if she had been ten years younger, came through a doorway and announced happily, "I'm Jennifer Sizemore and you are Mr…"

I stood up. "Chandler. Roy Chandler." I considered asking her for an ice-breaker if perchance she had been raised in Mineola and by chance was she the Jennifer who "sux dicks," but probably she wasn't. We shook hands and she led me down a tiled corridor and grandly ushered me into a brightly lit claustrophobic cubicle about four feet square furnished with two chairs separated by a narrow table. On one wall was a still life print of an arrangement of books and two pink roses in a vase.

"Please. Sit down, Roy," she told me invitingly.

I slid in behind one side of the desk hoping my breath did not still reek of stale liquor. She closed the door. A well-lit tomb. She studied my application, her fixed smile only rarely modifying to a frown. I tried not to breathe. Damn, I wished I'd bought some Certs! Finally she smoothed the application on the table. "So, Roy, you would like to be an editorial assistant. Why is that?"

"You've got to start somewhere," I replied with brutal honesty. I have since learned that honesty in a job interview is a grave mistake. The first inkling of that truth I learned that day, during that interview. If anyone wants a job, always lie.

"So that when a better job with a smaller house is offered in six months, our house will be on your resume," she led me smoothly.

"Well. I don't know who…"

"Neither do I. But some firm…Look, Roy. I started the same way. Personnel here wedged me into my current position. I wanted a career in publishing. When I got out of graduate school, I didn't want to spend my days interviewing mostly morons for jobs. I wanted to be a part of finding new talent. Have something to do with the great books of my lifetime." She fell silent and frowned at my application. "You've noted here that you have written a book that has been accepted for publication. Congratulations!"

"Thank you, but I just collaborated on it," I said modestly, my throat tightening, thinking of Fishbein. "We were colleagues in graduate school."

"You have listed a telephone number here, but no address," she remarked mildly.

"The telephone is for my father's house on Long Island. I was sharing an apartment with my collaborator but then…it was finished…The book was, I mean." God! Surely I wasn't going to start crying in front of this kindly inquisitor.

She looked up at the print on the wall and said, "I see. Now, Roy, we have an opening or two for assistants—we always do— and you are certainly well qualified, but the final decision is up to Mark Ripley, the director of personnel. As far as I can see, the only flaw is that you have written or, as you put it, collaborated on a book."

"Why is that a strike against me?"

"It's because you have probably developed a style of your own. The company likes unmolded clay, so to speak, people who can be trained to look for what the editors are wanting at a particular time. Believe me, it changes often. I will, of course, put your application on file. It should place you near the top of the pool." She smiled briefly.

"Thank you very much."

"I'm not certain I'm doing you any favor. If you take a position as an editorial assistant, my guess is you'll quit in three months." She rose and opened the door to the spacious telephone booth.

I cut over to Seventh Avenue. That wasn't bad for a cold call, I thought, but I needed to get methodical about job-hunting. And, by the way, I was walking to Seventh Avenue to search out a newsstand, to buy a *New York Times* in order to scan the help wanted ads, not for the girl in Sammy's joke who offered the blow-job. Believe me, I had one of those, under degrading circumstances that almost made up for the aching desire I had for the Fishbein I would probably never see again. And I didn't, save once, as I shall soon relate. It was years later.

It wasn't a newsstand that caught my attention. A branch of a big chain bookstore! And I saw a sign among the artfully displayed books which read:

EXPERIENCED HELP WANTED

Well? Why not? I had four years of experience as a retail clerk. Certainly I knew books. I could quickly thumb through *Books In Print*. This could be it! A hell of a lot more interesting than a copyreader for a publishing company. I went in and approached a nervous-looking, skinny, mousy-haired girl guarding the cash register.

"Excuse me. May I see the manager?"

"Oh dear! Yes, I suppose. Is something wrong?"

"Not that I know of. I want to check about the job." I pointed at the sign.

She relaxed. "I'll ring Mr. Goldfarb." After turning away, she spoke monosyllabically for a moment into the telephone receiver, apparently answering questions. Then she faced me and smiled tentatively. "He's coming now."

Sure enough, a tall, white-haired man, clenching in his jaw an unlit cigar the size of a horse turd and shrugging into an overcoat bustled toward me, an appraising expression on his face. He extended a well-manicured hand which I grasped in my untended one. "Jim Goldfarb."

"Roy Chandler."

"So," he said briskly, "you want to apply for a job?"

"Well, I'd like to know what the job is." I hoped I wasn't sounding too cocky. Apparently not.

"Aha! A young man who likes cards on the table. At the moment, it's assistant manager but, listen, I'm already late for a lunch meeting with the regional sales manager." He handed me a two-page application. "In the meantime you fill this out and I'll talk to you at one-thirty. Alice, let him use my office."

At the door, he turned back. "The key word is 'experienced,' Mr. Chandler, and that doesn't mean at shoeing horses or cleaning septic tanks. It means retail sales."

"Four years," I said.

"One-thirty, then," and he was gone.

The timid clerk, Alice, led me to the rear of the store. I asked, "What is he like? To work for?"

This Alice was no fool. Obviously she wasn't being considered for assistant manager, so there was a remote possibility that she was talking to her future supervisor. "He's very businesslike, but real fair. Expects you to be at work exactly on time. And he never makes passes at me." She giggled. "But you wouldn't be worried about that!"

After that morning I wasn't so sure. I thought uncharitably, not passes at you, maybe. I said, "Thanks, Alice."

This form was less interested in my health and more in my credentials. There was even a mini-aptitude test and questions, ridiculously easy ones, about books. One asked, "Who was the author of *The Sun Also Rises?*" It was even multiple choice.

While I waited for my interview, I browsed through the store, studied the layout, type-cast the clientele, noting that trade was not brisk. I wondered why an additional clerk was necessary.

* * * *

Mr. Goldfarb perused my application. "Well, well. An MFA. Very impressive!" He read on. "And you've written a book accepted for publication."

"Well, I co-authored it."

"You want a job here to push your own book when it is released?"

"Frankly, sir, after studying your customers for the past hour, I don't think any of them would want that book. It's mostly been businessmen after the *Wall Street Journal* or the *Times,* and file clerks buying Avalon romances to read on their lunch hours."

Mr. Goldfarb frowned. Had I been too blunt? He said, "That's one of the problems here. The location is lousy." A smile, then, "So how do you think four years of selling meat has prepared you for selling books?"

"I think sales of any retail product has a lot of aspects in common. You have to be pleasant and obliging and helpful without being glib or pushy."

He nodded, then asked suddenly, "If you were assistant manager what would be the first change you would suggest to me?"

I was ready for him. "There are really two of them. First, I'd recommend that the big 'special sale' sign come down."

"Why? Everyone likes a bargain."

"Not most people who buy books. Cut-rate prices mean second-rate books to them. Books are largely luxury items, but buyers don't expect to bargain for them like they would a Chrysler Imperial. Sure, discount books that are excess inventory or whatever the reason, but do it discreetly. Say someone picks up a book with a retail of $16.95. They want it, but…and then they see it's been marked down to $12.50. That's the sales clincher."

"Interesting," he said thoughtfully. "Worth a try. You said you had two ideas."

"Yes, sir. Over where the newspapers and magazines are isolated on racks, why not put some display tables? You know, current books on business and tax accounting under the *Wall Street Journal* for the businessmen and books on interior decorating and gardening under the racks for *House Beautiful,* and so on. A customer who comes in for a twenty-five cent newspaper or a dollar magazine may leave with a ten- or twenty-dollar book."

"Not bad. There's a reason why we keep books out of the newspaper and magazine section. Shoplifting."

"Mr. Goldfarb, I don't have any statistics, but I'd be willing to wager that—except for pornography stores—the shoplifting rate is lower in a bookstore than any kind of retail business."

He gazed at me momentarily before saying, "You have a job. Monday morning. Eight-thirty sharp. Any questions?"

I had plenty, but I started to ask, "How…?"

"One thousand per month, payable on the first and fifteenth. That was your question?"

"Yes, sir." Wow! What an answer!

"I thought so. Now let me give you some bad news. This store is currently operating in the red. That was one of the topics of discussion during my meeting with the regional manager. If it doesn't do a turnaround or at least break even by year's end, the branch will be closed in June when the lease expires. That may mean, repeat *may,* that you will be unemployed, but not necessarily. You could be transferred. See, I've also been given a highly profitable store on Lexington Avenue to manage. I expect to be spending most of my time there. Not likely I'll be here more than a day a week, so for all practical purposes you'll *be* the manager."

This is not a story about my career, but the skeletal facts bear upon the rest of the narrative. The store on Seventh Avenue did break even by the end of the year. I would like to claim some credit, but it may have just been the Christmas rush. Jim Goldfarb and I became great friends, in fact, we often had lunch together over the years and last April I was named an active pallbearer at his funeral. He never admitted it but I'm sure, when the company brass opted to close my store, despite a first quarter profit, it was he who was responsible for my being chosen as manager of the brand-new, shiny mall bookstore in Bethpage. For that matter when, two years later, I was made district manager over all eighteen Long Island stores with a new office over the shop in Huntington, possibly Jim had some influence. But by five years ago, when I was named Northeastern regional manager, Jim had retired.

The company brass keeps wondering why I insist on keeping the office in Huntington. After all, they tell me I could have an office in New York or Boston or Philadelphia. Who wouldn't want to live in a nice suburb? Have lunch at marvelous restaurants? Commute to the big city? Answer: me.

Then too, over the years, whenever a thin volume of poetry is published by Adeline Fishbein, I always send out a memo to my store and district managers instructing them to display and promote the title vigorously. The braver, or those who know me well, protest saying, "Poetry? That stuff is slow as shit on the market!"

I always blandly reply, "I know. I don't like it either but the author was a colleague of mine in graduate school. It's just for old times' sake."

And yes, the rumor is true, the higher up you are in a business and the more money you make, the less work you have to do. But, no, I won't tell you which bookstore chain employs me. Regional managers can get sacked, too.

Once out on the sidewalk, my thrill of conquest vanished. I was struck again by a saddening slap of rootlessness. Where should I go? The prospect of the overheated, worn Astoria apartment was intoxicatingly inviting. No, I was through there. I glumly shuffled over to 21st Street, bailed out my car and drove aimlessly around Manhattan, which is extraordinarily dangerous when one is absorbed in thought and remembrance.

I stopped at a bar in the upper west 60s only because there was a vacant parking space adjacent. It reminded me all too much of the establishment facing the Major Deegan Expressway where Fishbein and I had first drunk together, after my VW was stolen. I sipped a beer in deliberate thoughtlessness. When I paid I found the two cards in my wallet among the currency. Yes! That would decide it! A toss of the coin. Actually a great many coins for I would have to call long distance. Either it would be Rebecca or Christine Arthur. Simple!

I called Rebecca. She had an answering machine in operation. After the toneless sterile message and a beep, I said, "Rebecca! This is Roy Chandler. I need to talk to you. Call me at…at…" I briefly considered. It had to be Pop's number. I recited it an added, "This is important!" That was a stupid call. Rebecca would still be at work. Of course!

So, it would be Christine. I made the connection, but it was clearly not she who answered. A heavily accented, "Arthur resident. Hallo?"

"Miss Arthur, please. This is Roy Chandler calling."

"Not here. Sorry. Gone to city. Meeting with big bangers." It crossed my mind that Christine might not want it to be the knowledge of casual callers that she was meeting with the big "bangers."

"I see. Well, please tell her I called."

"Yes, Mr. Candle."

The hell with women! I'd just drive out to Pop's. And I did, pulling into the driveway behind the Lincoln, just as he was getting out of it. His face lit up with genuine pleasure. On impulse I leaped out of the car, ran to him and hugged him—something I hadn't done in ten years. I asked, "You interested in a bachelor roommate, Pop?"

"Sure I am! Funny thing, I bought a six-pack of beer just last night. I must have had a premonition. I've even got some beef stew in the freezer."

"The freezer?" I asked, following him into the kitchen. "Are we going to eat at midnight?"

Pop grinned, patted the top of the microwave—still something of a curiosity in 1975—and said, "The bachelor's companion. Get yourself a beer."

He put the plastic freezer container into the oven, set the timer and controls, then set about mixing his Scotch and water. Good old Pop, I thought, he would never dream of making the first inquiry as to the circumstances of my presence. If and when I chose to tell him any details, he would offer his undivided attention.

We settled at the kitchen table initially in companionable silence. Suddenly I realized how emotionally and physically exhausted I was. Pop just then observed, "You look beat."

I laughed. "I was just now feeling it. By the way, the book is finished and we've got a publisher."

"I know. Your mother told me."

"She did? You two are getting chummy. Thinking of retying the knot?"

"God, no! She's just concerned about you. I keep telling her you're a grown man. It's your life. But she won't leave it alone."

"Menopause?"

"Could be. She always held it up to me that the Whitcombs, her family, had held onto their money and the Chandlers blew theirs."

"They never had nearly as much. I'm sure you never gave the impression you had money."

"I tried not to, but she was determined to believe that a Brown graduate—even one who paid most of his college expenses thanks to the G.I. Bill—must be secretly rich." He laughed and asked suddenly, "Do you know how my father, your grandfather, died?"

"Not exactly. Just that he drowned."

"Drowned, yes. Trying to save the last symbol of the Chandler money. A seventy-two-foot motor yacht he had built in the Graves' Yard in Marblehead in 1928. It happened in 1953, during Hurricane Carol. He left the dockage at Cos Cob to allow plenty of sea room in the Sound. At some point he left the wheelhouse, was washed overboard, and *Symbolism* sank. Vanished. The name was ironic, because he died for the last symbol of Chandler money. And it was a sham."

"Why?"

"He left ten thousand dollars in debts, was posted at both the University Club and his yacht club. You were five before I got everything paid off."

"Is there a lesson in what you're telling me?"

"Not really, except be yourself. The sixty-five thousand I have in permanent savings is in CDs or tax-exempts, it's real. I've got nothing to show off, or to hide."

"Incidentally I have a new job. What Mother would call a 'decent' job."

"Really? I thought perhaps you'd become a professional writer now."

I shook my head. "Not me. I was operating under orders. If I ever write again it will be strictly for pleasure and I don't think that's the way to vast riches. No, starting Monday I'm the assistant manager of a bookstore on Seventh Avenue."

"Do you think you'll enjoy that?"

"If I don't, I'll quit. But at the moment I'm sort of excited. Can you drop me at the station in the mornings? It makes more sense to take the train than to drive."

"Sure, Roy. No problem. Get another beer."

So it was that for a month I became a book-selling, Long Island Rail Road commuting, eunuch. On Sunday I went to Mother's to gather the businessman's trappings she had bought me and which I had previously shunned. She was thrilled about my new job and guardedly pleased that I was going to be living with Pop. That is, she said, "Anything would be an improvement."

On impulse, I stopped at Zuma Alcorn's on my way back to Mineola. As soon as I was seated and she had hungrily seized and lit one of my cigarettes, she said, "So, it didn't work out. Fishbein, I mean."

"No it didn't. How did you know?"

"She was here. Just left a few minutes ago. She really is broken up about it." In the winter afternoon light, despite her handsome features, she looked all her seventy-five years. "I'd hoped that you two could make a go of it."

"Well, Mother's certainly pleased," I said grimly, "and it wasn't my fault. Did she...did Fishbein say it was?"

"No, but I could tell she was devastated. When she was leaving she said, 'It was only possible with Chandler,' or words to that effect."

I was silent a moment, forcing back emotion, choking down tears. "She was abused as a child by a mother who committed suicide. It warped her, made her unable to love in the completely normal sense of the word." I spoke woodenly.

"That explains a lot," she said finally.

I got up, "It explains a lot...and nothing."

*****

The routine that Pop and I established was simple. Each morning we arose at seven, performed our ablutions, breakfasted and talked about the news, most of which, in late 1975, was bad. Then Pop drove me to the commuter train station and was waiting for me in the evenings upon my return from the city. Usually at night, I went for long walks, sometimes to the park of my youth, occasionally past the handsome Arthur residence with its "For Sale" and later "Sold" signs. And often I just walked aimlessly. Once a silver Camaro slowed as it passed by but did not stop. A few times Pop accompanied me, but it was rare. He sensed, astutely, that I wanted to be alone with my reminiscences and healing the scars of the Fishbein affair. Sometimes I was sad, on occasion angry. Why had I not had the strength to dominate the love? Why did anyone have to be dominant in a romance? I never received answers. Nor did I receive answering calls from either Rebecca or Christine. Had I become a social pariah?

I called Rebecca one night. After several rings a tentative, "Hello."

"Rebecca?"

"Oh. Hi, Roy. I've been wanting to call you, but I've had trouble getting up the nerve." Her voice was lethargic.

"Nerve? I didn't know I was so unapproachable."

"You are. Now."

"I wasn't one night, I vividly recall," I said, which was the wrong quip. She burst into tears.

Finally, I said, "Cheer up, I must have enjoyed it or I wouldn't be calling you now."

"No, Roy. It would be hopeless after I let Fishbein debase me. And you. I loved you so much, Roy!"

"You don't now?"

"Yes, but it would never be the same. That…bitch ruined it for me! For us. She knew what she was doing!" Then more quietly, "I gave Sterling notice yesterday. I'm moving back to Jersey; I'll work in one of Daddy's stores until I can find something better."

"So you don't want to see me again?"

"Part of me is desperate to, but I just can't. Roy, will you do me a favor?"

"Name it."

"Don't think of me when I was in bed. Remember me as the polite young lady you took to meet your wonderful father."

I choked out, "I will. Goodbye."

And that was the last contact I had with Rebecca although, as I've mentioned, she came back to the city—to work, at least. She is still beautiful or the television make-up artists are masters.

One Saturday morning, just before Christmas, I found it had snowed during the night and become bitterly cold. Pop poured coffee for me and said, "It's down to twenty degrees. If you plan to go for a walk, better wrap up."

"I will. Want to come along?"

"Not me. You're the masochist in the house. It's days like this when I wish the house had been built with a fireplace."

"You could have one put in."

"And fiddle-fuck with firewood? Forget it."

"How about a set of gas logs in it?"

"Hmm. Not bad. I'll think about it."

"Incidentally, Pop, we ought to discuss money."

"Why? Do you need some?"

"No, of course not. But it seems like I ought to contribute something toward expenses. Outside of commuting, I haven't spent more than twenty dollars a week. The book advance and Sammy's last check I put in a CD, but I still have nearly two thousand in my checking account."

Pop said, "Saving money is a good habit. I suppose you could buy your own beer. Everything else I'd have to buy anyway."

That came as a small shock. During that month I had been so introspective, I had not even realized where the beer I drank had been coming from. "Sure, I will. And Scotch for you, too."

Outside, the snowfall had ceased and watery winter sun was piercing the iron-gray clouds. Had there been a breeze, walking would have been out of the question. I had donned a crew-neck sweater and my fleece-lined rawhide coat.

Walking toward the park, I decided to make a New Year's resolution to forget the past and concentrate on the present, plan for the future. Unfortunately, the present—except for the comfort of living with Pop and my store saving efforts—was bleak.

Mousy little Alice, at the store, had begun to make overtures toward me. Often she came to work wearing make-up for which I complimented her and not wearing a bra which I didn't mention. On the no-bra days she made a conscious effort to bend over, when I was in her vicinity, to reveal her small, uninteresting breasts and tiny pink nipples. I guessed I was spoiled. Once I did speculate whether her pubic hair was as sparse as Sally Becker's, but quickly drove the comparison from my mind.

Once at the park, I dusted the snow from my favorite bench and the engraving, "Jennifer sux dicks," and sat down. My present life "sux dicks" I thought morosely.

Then, a new silver Camaro crunched to a stop at the snowy curb and my life changed forever. I didn't realize it at that minute, of course. Owing to the snow I did not hear her approach. Initially I had glanced over and noted a woman get out, probably youngish, but it was impossible to tell with her heavily quilted blue parka and baggy flannel jogging pants. I returned to my unhappy thoughts. Her voice was sharp and so close it startled me. "You don't need to ignore me, Roy Chandler. It looks like our paths are going to keep crossing so we may as well make the best of it."

"Christine!" I leaped up and hugged her. "I guessed you were back in Virginia. When I called and left a message, your Sri Lankan or Lithuanian or whatever cleaning woman told me you were in the city with some big New York 'bangers.'" I imitated the woman. "I didn't think you were interested in an ordinary banger like me. You never called back. Then I saw the house was sold." I shrugged then brushed off more of the snow and said, "Sit down."

"The fool woman never told me. It seems like our whole lives have been a string of broken communication." She took my gloved hand in hers and laughed.

"Remember the movie *Cool Hand Luke?* Where the prison guard kicks Paul Newman in the face and says, 'What we have here is a failure to communicate'?"

"Why are you still here? Where are you staying?"

"Jesus, Roy! It's been a tangled mess. I had to sell out my business. I've rented a house in Merrick."

"How did you know to look for me here?"

"I called your father. For the last couple of weeks I've been seeing two cars in your driveway. I couldn't think of any reason for him to have two cars, so I called. He told me I'd probably find you here, that you came here often to think.

"He's right about that. I do."

"What do you think about?"

"About how sorry I'm feeling for myself."

"How is your affair you mentioned?"

"About as cold as this park bench. It was, without boring you with any grim details, a fucking disaster."

A small voice, "Oh. Do you ever think about me?"

"Very often." I smiled. "And once in a while," pointing to the graffiti behind me, "I wonder about Jennifer here who 'sux dicks.'"

"Ha! That's one former imponderable I can lay to rest for you. Her name was Jennifer Teague and by reputation, it was fully accurate. It's possible she carved it herself. The last I heard of her she was a graduate student at Emory University in Atlanta studying comparative religions."

"You're freezing," I observed. She was shaking and her lips were blue-white.

"Let's go sit in the car."

She started the engine and switched on the heater fan, then turned to face me. By unspoken accord, we leaned toward the center of the car and, just over the console and the shift lever, we kissed.

Drawing back, I said, "This is just a fancy Volkswagen." And we laughed.

A thought came to my thawing brain. "Christine, why are you having to do everything to settle the estate? You have parents, don't you? Wasn't he your father's father?"

A blank look, then disbelief, then, "Roy! Are you crazy? They're both dead! They died while I was in college. That's what hurt me so much—broke my heart—that you didn't write; even send a sympathy card! Of course, now I know why. Cornell was classes and funerals for me."

I took her hand, "Was it an accident?"

"Oh, no. You never met Mother or Father, but they were both well past forty when I was born. They developed various medical problems. Mother died my freshman year and Father during the summer before I was a senior. I hope my grandfather's longevity counts for something on my heredity chart."

"I'm sorry. I just didn't know."

She leaned over and gave me a quick kiss. "Don't be. I'm all well now. How would you like to come over to Merrick tonight? We could talk about old times. Maybe relive some of them," she added, raising one suggestive eyebrow.

"No," I said, "I have a better idea. I'm taking you out to dinner tonight. Talking and reliving old times will be on New Year's Eve. That is, if you're free."

"All right with me, but why, Roy?"

"It has to do with an amendment of a resolution I made to myself just an hour ago, walking over here."

"Which was?"

"To forget the past, make the best of the present and plan for a better future. The last two I'm still all for. The past I'm willing to rethink."

"Why?"

My answer surprised me. "Partly because of you, which makes me remember all the good things in my life. Early recollections here. Growing up on City Island. College. Working at crazy Sammy's butcher shop. Times I've laughed until my stomach hurt. Sag Harbor! Screwing in the Volkswagen! Am I being corny?"

"No, Roy. You're telling me ways people learn to love. My parents were too old to know how to bring me up, to understand a child, or an adolescent. But at least they loved me, so I know how to love. Now I'm sounding corny as hell."

"Why shouldn't we? Who's to hear? Christine, I once knew a girl who couldn't love. Not the way we're talking about. Oh, sure, she could fuck all night. But, she never could love. Not in the spiritual way. See, she was horribly abused as a child. Never learned how to handle a true relationship." I was amazed I had gotten through the monologue with no show of emotion.

"Was this your recent affair?"

"Yes. Fishbein." Now my emotions were dealing cards.

Christine sensed that and said, "I'll drive you home. I'd like to meet your father."

Christine made a cautious U-turn and then said, "What do you do? I mean for a job."

"I am assistant manager of a bookstore in the city which may be closed in six months unless it starts making a profit and then I'll most likely be unemployed. If there was someone to ask for their blessing in any hypothetical plans for matrimony and that someone asked me, 'What are your prospects, young man?' I would have to say 'lousy.' It's lucky the bride-elect is a wealthy heiress."

A cross between a snort and a laugh sounded. "Wealthy, hell! If you're hypothetically marrying me, let me clear the air. As of last Thursday, I'm through with big 'bangers.' My account has been credited with the vast sum of $233,000."

"Really! I'd have guessed the house alone was worth nearly $150,000. Still you're not exactly a pauper."

"No," she said, "but it should have been more. Grandfather didn't really keep up with his investments the last few years. I sold the house for $142,000 only to find out there was a $60,000 mortgage to be satisfied. It seems his accountant screwed up and there were all kinds of back taxes and penalties, so Grandfather took out a mortgage. I'm not complaining. There is still a little of Father's money left, too."

*****

Pop stood in the doorway looking stunned. Christine had removed her coat and was shaking the snow from her long, blond hair. "Pop? Are you all right? Where are the manners you taught me? I said this is Christine Arthur."

"My God!" he said, "She not only changed her name, she's changed colors!"

"What the hell…" I turned toward Christine who now stood primly erect, a calm smile concealing her perplexion. Pop was right! Except for the color of her eyes and skin, Christine's features and figure and carriage were the image of Rebecca Albritton. To me, each was so totally a different person, I would never had noticed the least similarity. In a way, I wished Pop hadn't.

Mother was ecstatic about our engagement and insisted upon running announcements in all the newspapers. In response, I received the photograph, or a copy, of Fishbein in the nude, which had hung above the stereo in the Astoria apartment. At the bottom, inscribed in her flowing script, I read:

> *Chandler,*
> *Congratulations!*
> *The side of me you could love and*
> *loved you back.*
> *Lili Marlene*

It hangs over my desk in the study. Perhaps I ought to take it down since the children are getting old enough to take an interest in it. But I probably won't. Christine has never been critical of it.

Fishbein, by the way, in addition to her books of poetry has made quite a reputation for herself in the music world, having written the lyrics to several musical scores. She has never married.

*****

For a wedding present, Mother insisted upon sending us to Bermuda for our honeymoon. Her sage remark was, "Get the marriage off to a positive start." What an authority!

I've never told her it was merely happenstance that her earlier censoriousness didn't preclude the ultimate union. What would be the point? She has never made the connection between the Christine of the letters and Christine the wife. I have never told her. Again, what would be the point?

Except for "Pop's Month" we go to City Island one Sunday a month for fricasseed children and usually stop at McDonald's on the way home. Now that the children are old enough that they don't bother her "things," Mother seems to rather like them. Christy was born when we had been married just three years and Artie followed two years later. It seems we aren't very imaginative when it comes to names.

One Sunday, not long ago, Mother pulled me aside out of Christine's earshot, as though my wife of many years was a scheming gigolet, and said, "I find that I have nearly two million dollars in assets not including the house and my interest in the business which, except for a generous bequest to my church, is willed to you."

"Thanks, Mother, but I'm doing quite well. Don't kick off on my account." Who knows? Maybe there will again be, someday, Chandler money worth talking about.

Mother is sixty-nine. Lately, she says with conviction, "Next year, when I'm seventy, I definitely am going to retire." She says it with almost the same adamancy that—five years ago—she insisted, "Next year, when I am sixty-five, I am going to retire."

She still drives a zero- to five-year-old Pontiac with all the hubcaps intact, except for the 1980 model that was heartlessly rammed by an ignominious garbage truck. That's Mother.

*****

"Pop's Month," is August. It is then when he leaves the guest cottage of Uncle Manny's estate overlooking the Loxahatchee River and comes north. The first and last week he stays with us, with two sandwiched weeks when we all go out to Sag Harbor.

He adores the children, spoils them at times, I'm afraid.

After our Bermuda honeymoon, we began our housekeeping in Christine's rented tract house in Merrick. Upon my managerial promotion to Bethpage, we negotiated with the owner and subsequently bought the house. When Pop retired seven years ago, he insisted upon deeding over the Mineola house to us. Since the children were growing, we moved into it because there was a fourth bedroom and two full baths.

The first summer Pop came I offered him our bedroom but he refused, opting for the little bedroom of my childhood. I asked him why. "What goes around comes around, they say. I'm not sure exactly what that means so let me simplify it by just saying I want to enjoy the irony of visiting this house with a happy family living in it."

When my biography of Zuma Alcorn was finished—I rushed it, guilty because it would be posthumous—I called it *Three Little Words*. The editor of the publishing house which accepted it told me: "The only problem is the title sucks. You've got the famous Zuma Alcorn for a subject. It has to be in the title."

"What do you want to call it?" I asked.

"*The Ultimate Rainbow: Zuma Alcorn's Life*. Catchy, isn't it?"

"If you say so," I said. So, I'm giving *Three Little Words* a third try. Perhaps three is the magic number. *The Ultimate Rainbow* sold rather briskly because the great lady had so recently died and the critics were kind. The best review I received was in an unsigned note which came to my office in Huntington. It read:

> *Chandler:*
> *I told you that you could write.*
> *Half of all my love.*

*****

It is to this day painful, but I will retell it: about the last—only—time I saw Fishbein after our breach. Often, between Mother's unsatisfying chicken fricassee and McDonald's and Mineola, we stopped to visit Zuma Alcorn. This particular incidence was some three months before the grand woman's death.

As we departed, walking along the sidewalk toward the driveway where our Volvo was parked, a woman stepped from a white Buick sedan pulled up to the curb. She wore a trim green suit and was exquisitely Fishbein. She approached us and said brightly, "Why, Mr. and Mrs. Chandler! How are you? And Christy and Artie! So nice to see you! You're certainly growing well and healthy."

"Nice to see you," I said numbly.

Fishbein passed on to Zuma Alcorn's door and was admitted. Christine looked after her. The children had run ahead to establish back seat positions. Fighting ensued.

"What a beautiful woman!" Christine exclaimed. "Really striking!"

"Yes. Striking. She said that once."

Our eyes met over and across the roof of the car. Christine noted the tears flowing down my cheeks and said sympathetically, "So that was Fishbein."

"Yes. Lili Marlene."

The End